Bitter Bonds

Heather Osborne

This is a work of fiction. Names, characters, places, and incidents are either the product of the author's imagination or used fictitiously, and any resemblance to actual people, alive or dead, business, establishments, locales, or events is entirely coincidental.

Any reference to real events, businesses, or organizations is intended to give the fiction a sense of realism and authenticity.

ISBN-13: 978-1530139323
ISBN-10: 1530139325

Cover Design by Victoria Cooper Art

Edited by Susie McKinstray

Any errors are the sole responsibility of the author.

Dedication

To the dreamers, lovers, and
adventurers of this world.

Never stop seeking personal happiness.

Part I

"I never think of the future ...
but am determined to make the most of the present."
~ *Charlotte Temple*

1

May, 1834
Jefferson Parish, Louisiana

"A commoner? Father, you do realize our family can be traced back to the echelons of European royalty? You still correspond with relatives in England and France." Francine Beaumont was hardly ready to lay down her virginity for a man who bought his way into high society.

"What a despicable thing to say about a man you do not know. Besides, he can offer you a large plantation, slaves, and wealth. We are faltering, my dear. Certainly you have seen how household expenses have been cut in the past year," Lord Arnaud Beaumont admonished his eldest daughter.

Francine had spurned nearly every suitor placed

in her path, but now it was time to marry off the bane of his existence. How had something so vicious spawned from such a gentle-born woman as Francine's mother? If only she were living now. Perhaps genial Marie would have been able to calm their daughter's ire.

"It is tantamount to selling *me* off to the highest bidder, Papa!" Francine attempted to use the childhood endearment so often uttered by her much more pliable sister.

"The matter is settled!" Lord Beaumont pounded his fist on the top of the polished desk, causing Francine to flee the room in tears, past her younger sister, Adrienne. She watched the retreating form of Francine for a few moments, before creeping into her father's study.

Arnaud was relieved to see his sweet, patient daughter appear in the doorway. Her pleasant face was encircled with golden ringlets, her clear, blue eyes full of love and concern. Adrienne, his pride and joy, so much like her mother in every way, would never have protested an arranged marriage. She would have considered it her honor, and duty, to oblige. She was the opposite, in every way, to her tantruming sister.

"Papa, you mustn't let Francine trouble you. Remember your constitution…" Adrienne had always been aware of the troubles plaguing her father. They had caused him to suffer horribly with stomach pains, only recently diagnosed as ulcerous. She knew Francine had no idea, nor would she care.

"*Ma petite*, you are too kind. If only it were you who Henri Du Cormier sought."

Seventeen-year old Adrienne was already well-versed in the matters of arranged marriage. However, she knew she had more chance of marrying for love than her titled, elder sister. Francine looked upon Adrienne with contempt, envying her freedom, however minute.

"Papa, if I could, I would gladly take her place. Why does Monsieur Du Cormier seek a bride with a title? Surely such things do not matter here anymore." Louisiana was a part of the United States. The French Revolution had dispatched with the monarchy, and the British held no control over them. Titles were obsolete relics of the past.

Arnaud rubbed the bridge of his nose, removing his silver-rimmed spectacles, and closing his doleful chocolate brown eyes. His graying, dark brown hair only betrayed his age. "I wish I knew, *ma petite*. He came into this money suddenly, only able to buy St. Esprit through sheer luck! I wish it were different. My title, therefore Francine's, is useless."

Adrienne crossed the room, kneeling at her father's side, no care that she wrinkled her carefully pressed silk gown. "Mayhap we could speak to him? Surely he would not want such a wife as Francine, once he sees her ways."

"Francine would never disgrace herself by behaving poorly at a public function, especially with the height of society attending." Arnaud shuffled some papers aside. "It would alleviate my anguish greatly if you were to find a husband, someone to make you completely happy beyond your wildest dreams."

Smiling warmly, Adrienne gazed up at her mother's portrait above the fireplace. Marie was captured in the prime of youth and beauty. She saw her mother's features in herself, knowing this was why her father favored her so. "You mean like how you were with Mama?"

Arnaud lifted his gaze, peering up at his beloved. They had grown up in a tumultuous world in pre-revolutionary France, hiding their aristocratic upbringing. When Arnaud had prospered in the shipping business, the young couple made their way to the French-owned Louisiana territory. How they celebrated when the United States bought it, knowing their daughters would grow up in a free country.

Adrienne was three when their mother passed away from consumption. She vaguely remembered the tender-hearted woman, who had soothed her nightmares with soft, French lullabies. Often, her dreams were full of the music, as she twirled her small fingers into the woman's blonde ringlets. She felt cheated not to have spent more time with her mother, but guilty for those feelings at the same time.

Finally, Arnaud spoke, "Yes, like how I was with Mama. I wish she were here. She had a way with Francine. Francine would throw the most violent tantrums, sending nannies and maids running from the nursery. Marie walked in, composed, and quieted the storm."

Before melancholy could descend over the pair, Adrienne changed the subject. "Helene says everything is prepared for this evening. All the silver is polished, and the ballroom floor has been swept and cleaned. She wanted me to ask your approval on the canapés."

Patting his daughter's hand, Arnaud left the final

touches to Adrienne. “I am sure what you decide will be scrumptious. Is she preparing a full course meal, or a buffet?”

“She thought it best to provide guests with titbits of food, right in the ballroom. It’s very new-fangled. I believe I will ask for the salmon and dill. It is my favorite, after all.” Adrienne rose, brushing the fabric of her pale pink dress.

“I leave it all in your more than capable care, *ma petite*. Now, hurry along, and reassure Helene. I am sure she will be beside herself, wondering what my decision shall be.” Arnaud winked and stood, placing a doting kiss on his daughter’s brow.

“I will, Papa.” Adrienne exited the room in a rustle of skirts, her heels clicking delicately on the wooden floor.

Arnaud sat down again, pressing his hand to his stomach to find some relief from the gurgling sensation building there. He slid open a drawer in his desk, and took a dose of the prescribed laudanum. Reclining back in the chair, he waited for the pain to recede, praying to his long silent God that Francine would do something for the family, for once in her life.

“Helene?” Adrienne poked her head into the kitchen, breathing in the smell of freshly baked honey bread. “Mmmm!” She crept over to the place where the bread was cooling, and reached to break off a chunk.

“Mademoiselle Adrienne! That is for the midday meal! I have a fresh pot of stew bubblin’ away.”

Helene bustled from the pantry, wiping her hands on her worn apron.

Snatching her hand back, Adrienne smiled warmly at the old cook. Helene had been there as long as she could remember, with her kind, brown eyes and work-worn features; always stern but kind. "I am sorry, Helene. Papa asked me to come down, and say the salmon and dill will be fine for the canapés."

"Well, it's about time! I've been frettin' for hours! Now, shoo. You'll want to have a rest before the guests descend on us like a holy plague!" Helene ushered Adrienne out of the kitchen, but not before slipping a fresh, honey bread roll into her hand. "Don't you say I'm never good to you, missy!" Her eyes crinkled as she smiled.

Adrienne felt the warm confection in her hand, and ascended the stairs, only to be met at the top by Francine, green eyes red-rimmed from her heart-wrenching sobs. "What were you doing down there?"

"I was delivering a message from Father about the hors d'oeuvres for tonight," Adrienne spoke carefully, knowing her sister was quick to anger. She still felt the sting of many hair pulls from their childhood. She secreted her prize in the folds of her skirt with subtle movements, knowing Francine would steal it, if given the chance.

"Tonight? You mean the evening where my life comes to an end? Where I am forced to marry a man I know nothing about?" Francine, ever the expert in dramatics, slumped delicately against the wall.

Drawing in a shaky breath, Adrienne strove to soothe her sister. "Have you met him yet? Perhaps he is devastatingly handsome."

"How could he be? He is not from *our* class of people!" Francine flounced off down the hall, punctuating her flight with more sobs.

Adrienne shook her head. Francine would surely bring the entire mood of the house to a head. Everyone would be on edge, worried about upsetting their volatile charge. Bringing her treat once more back into sight, Adrienne pressed her nose to the top, breathing in the sweet smell and biting into it, letting the flavors fill her senses. Maybe this marriage to Henri Du Cormier would be good for all of them, if it got Francine out of their lives.

The evening arrived swiftly. Adrienne stood proudly by her father's side as hostess, as Francine was too sulky to perform the duty. Her new dress was the color of the midnight sky, lit by a full moon. It fell in soft waves down the full skirt, accented by white lace. Her gloves were of the best quality, and her hair was styled meticulously. Despite the financial troubles, Arnaud always managed to dress his daughters to their standing.

Francine was a contrast to her sister, choosing a low-cut bodice, almost daring. Her emerald dress mimicked her disagreeable personality, and she chose black accents, instead of the more delicate white. Her ebony hair was upswept in corkscrew curls around her pinched face. There was no persuading her otherwise. She maintained her position in the ballroom, away from the arriving guests, seething in silent rage. *When was this Du Cormier meant to arrive?* She pondered this question over and over, wanting to do something to dissuade him, but not wanting to ruin her name in the process.

"Francine, darling! You look...divine!" Rosalind Denis floated towards her in a decadent creation of burgundy.

One of Francine's only friends, the woman was quick to confide in her. "Rosalind, darling, something horrible has happened!"

"Oh my, do tell." Rosalind flicked open her fan, surveying the entering guests, and attempting to discern who the eligible bachelors were. Her hazel eyes scanned the room eagerly, using a free hand to gently puff her coiffed blonde hair.

Francine drew her attention back, exasperated at the lack of sympathy from her friend. "I am to be married."

"Married? But isn't that wonderful? You will have your own household, and expenditures. It will be sublime."

Francine opened her mouth to protest, but then pressed the full lips together. Du Cormier had come into money; a great sum, if rumors were to be believed. "Oh, I did not consider this."

"Of course not, my dear. You were thinking with your heart. Foolish, really." Rosalind returned to her perusal of the men.

Francine balked at the accusation. "Foolish? My heart? I fear you've confused me with Adrienne."

"Who is your betrothed then?"

"Nothing is formal yet. It is Henri Du Cormier."

Rosalind's eyes went like saucers, and she

snapped her fan closed. "Oh my, aren't we the lucky one? Did you know he recently bought St. Esprit, with all the slaves, and money to spare? The previous owner, sadly, was a gambler. I don't blame him. His wife ran off with some merchant." She prattled on about the scandal, but Francine was no longer listening. She had to make Du Cormier love her, no matter what.

Adrienne glanced over her shoulder, watching Francine conspire with Rosalind. Each was as bad as the other. The sound of her father's rumbling voice uttering a familiar name, had her turning her head. The new arrival did not go unnoticed, as a hush fell over the room.

"Monsieur Du Cormier, such a pleasure to see you again. May I present my daughter, Adrienne?"

Henri Du Cormier wasn't like any knight in shining armor. His features were plain, intensified by high cheekbones, and a square jaw. He had long, black hair pulled back in a queue, and dark gray eyes that seemed to pierce her very soul, bringing a blush to her cheeks.

"Monsieur, welcome to our home."

Henri took the delicate beauty's hand, pressing his lips to the back. "A pleasure, mademoiselle."

Francine huffed in indignation from across the room. She was not going to let Adrienne steal this man's attentions. She pranced over, pushing her sister aside. "Monsieur! So sorry I was detained. I am Francine Beaumont." She held out her hand expectantly, carefully perusing his appearance. She did not care much for the facial hair, but that was something she could easily change, once they were married.

Adrienne wisely chose the moment to retreat, leaving the perplexing man to her sister. She did not want a husband she had to decipher on a daily basis. Simple, loving, and kind was more than enough for her.

2

Henri Du Cormier had no idea what to expect when he arrived by carriage at the lavish Beaumont plantation. The tree-lined drive, as well as waiting valets and slaves, told him he really had arrived in a different kind of society. Descending from his conveyance, Henri was ushered through the entry, and to the ballroom, where music was provided by a delicate string quartet. As he approached the host, his attention was drawn to the beauty in blue standing beside Lord Beaumont.

Henri knew he was not the most attractive of men. Many women found his dark manner off-putting, but fascinating. This young lady barely flinched when he was introduced. However, there was hardly any time to speak, as she was unceremoniously brushed aside by another woman, nearly of equal beauty. With mild disappointment, he learned this was Francine Beaumont, his soon-to-be fiancée.

"Quite a pleasure, Mademoiselle Beaumont," Henri greeted her, putting on every ounce of charm he possessed. As the woman fawned over him, he stole glances around for the golden-haired goddess who had captivated him so, but she had vanished from sight.

"Tell me, monsieur, I hear you have purchased St. Esprit. Is it to your liking? I have never been there myself." Her décolletage dipped low, almost to an indecent level.

Henri coughed. "Yes, mademoiselle. It is very nice. Unfortunate business though, purchasing the plantation. It should not be discussed in front of a lady."

Tittering, Francine flicked open her fan. "Oh, you do go on, sir."

Swallowing back an uneasy lump forming in his throat, Henri guided Francine over to the buffet table, piled high with wonderful smelling delicacies. "May I get you some champagne while you have something to eat?" Before she could respond, he moved away rapidly to find the drinks.

Francine watched his retreating back with disgust, stuffing a chocolate into her mouth. "Hrumph!"

Henri paid little attention to the woman he left, the first in a long line of slights she would end up holding against him. He did not know it at the time, but he had unleashed a horrible beast. As he sought out a slave balancing a tray of champagne flutes on his white-gloved hand, Henri noticed the bobbing head of the sister of his nearly betrothed returning to her father's side. Her hand delicately touched the old man's forearm, and Henri watched Lord Beaumont's face soften. Clearly, the young lady was a favorite.

Swiftly plucking two glasses from the tray, Henri returned to Francine, noting a small crumb on the corner of her mouth. Rejecting all thoughts of the youngest Beaumont daughter, he brushed it aside, handing her a glass. "Tell me, what do you enjoy doing, mademoiselle?"

Francine, placated by the gesture, delicately sipped from the crystal. "Oh, the usual lady's accomplishments. Music, art, needlepoint."

"Ah, I see. Do you read much?"

Scoffing, Francine quaffed the rest of the expensive beverage. "Read? Oh, no. I find such pursuits beyond a lady of quality. Ladies should be versed in the finer things in life, such as running a household, and playing the role of gracious hostess. Do you not agree?"

No, I certainly do not agree. Henri coughed into the back of his hand. "Er, yes, quite so." The quickly assembling guests were eyeing him with curiosity, and suspicion. Unacquainted with many of them, he knew he would have to make connections soon, if he were to remain in their good graces. Holding out his arm, Henri did his best to smile congenially at Francine. "Shall we take a turn around the room? I would very much like introductions to the guests, if you would be so kind?"

Francine's mouth opened and closed in an unladylike manner, before she transformed into all smiles again. "Why, yes, I think that would be quite agreeable." She placed a hand through his arm, drawing him close.

Henri felt the champagne rise into his gullet, but he was determined to make the most of his self-imposed situation. If only he had had the foresight to meet the family first, prior to agreeing to marry the eldest daughter of the Beaumont family. If he were to back out now, all his prospects would go with him. Henri did not think Francine was the forgiving sort. He reluctantly allowed himself to be hauled around the ballroom, all the while keeping one eye on the woman he truly desired.

Once all the guests were situated in the ballroom, Adrienne dismissed herself from her father's side. Seeking out her dearest friend from the neighboring plantation, she immediately pulled her aside for a clandestine conversation.

Elizabeth Forrest, Bessie to her friends, was also the youngest child in her family, however she was preceded by six brothers, all intelligent and happily married. Unfortunately, the downside to having so many elder siblings was no one was ever good enough for dear Bessie. She resigned herself to forever being a spinster, despite Adrienne's assurances no one could be so drastic at seventeen.

Tonight, her friend wore a peach-colored gown, which set off her mousy brown ringlets, with curling ribbons along her pale cheeks. Bessie clasped her friend's hands eagerly, having waited some time to confer with Adrienne.

"He seems rather put out, does he not?" Bessie drew Adrienne's arm through hers, and the two circled the ballroom, heads bent together.

Adrienne peered around, catching the eye of Monsieur Du Cormier briefly, and blushing furiously. "I find him very difficult to decipher presently."

Bessie laughed, patting her friend's arm. "You hate anything, and anyone, you cannot understand in an instant, Addy."

Worrying her lower lip between her straight, white teeth, Adrienne conceded her friend's point. She did thoroughly dislike cryptic people, and considered it a gift to understand someone's motivations and emotions from the outset. "It is true. He does perplex me. Did you notice how he keeps staring at me?"

"Be careful. If Francine picks up on his ulterior motives, you may be in for a hellish season," Bessie tutted gently. Many times she had visited the Beaumont Plantation, to hear Francine cursing her younger sister for some miniscule slight.

Adrienne inclined her head, knowing Bessie's words were full of truth. Francine would be vicious if she believed Adrienne rivaled her for Du Cormier's affections. "I will simply need to make it clear I do not return the man's affections, should it come to that." She raised her chin an inch, quite certain of herself.

Bessie laughed. "As you say, Addy."

"Ah, there you are, *ma petite*." Arnaud crossed the short distance to the pair. "Bessie! You look as lovely as ever!" He patted her cheek dotingly.

"Thank you, Lord Beaumont." Bessie bobbed her head in a slight curtsey.

Arnaud faced his daughter. "Would you do me

the honor of opening the dancing? Francine seems quite taken with Monsieur Du Cormier, thank God." Tension had slipped from his face in the past hour, pleased Francine had not rejected Du Cormier outright.

"Of course, Papa." Adrienne pressed her cheek to Bessie's. "We will speak later."

"Until then," Bessie murmured back, sighing softly as she watched Adrienne depart. Her father had been dead for five years, and she looked upon Lord Beaumont as a surrogate. She hoped desperately that Francine would finally leave them in peace.

Arnaud leaned his head down. "Were you and Bessie conspiring against some poor gentleman in the room?"

Adrienne squeezed her father's arm affectionately. "Oh, never, Papa. Don't you know you're the only man for me?"

Laughing, he spun his daughter out, taking the position for the opening waltz. "Someday, another man will replace me in your heart."

"Never!" Adrienne laughed, as the music struck up.

Rosalind weaseled her way back to Francine's side, taking in her friend's petulant expression, as she watched her father and sister dance. "Well?"

Slapping her fan closed, Francine scowled. "Well, what?"

Rolling her eyes dramatically, Rosalind gestured to Du Cormier, who was deep in conversation with

Bessie's eldest brother, George, the current master of Belle Rivière Plantation. There was a time Francine pursued him, but he was won over by the wispy Sarah Dixon from New York. Little hope existed now she was heavily pregnant with their first child. "Maybe she will die..." Francine muttered to herself.

"What was that?"

Francine jumped. "Nothing. Monsieur Du Cormier is polite enough, so it seems. He was attentive, for the most part." The waltz ended, and cordial applause filled the room. Couples made their way to the main floor for the next dance. She glanced around for Du Cormier, still deep in conversation with George.

"Attentive, hmm?" Rosalind smirked, fanning herself delicately. "Indeed."

"Oh, do shut up," Francine hissed venomously, jealousy rising, as a handsome young man led her younger sister to the floor. As if sensing his soon-to-be betrothed's ire, Du Cormier raised his eyes. Abruptly, Francine was all smiles, waving delicately.

"Well, I never! Here he comes. He certainly wants to win you over." Rosalind floated away, before Francine could let loose another barb. She had had enough of the spiteful woman for one evening.

Du Cormier bowed. "Apologies, mademoiselle. I found myself so swept up in the conversation, I neglected you shamefully. Please, would you care to dance?"

Smug in her victory, Francine took his offered hand. Although she would forgive him this slight, for the moment, she would tuck it away with the others of the evening, until they were wed. Then he would suffer for all the embarrassments she was made to endure.

3

The evening air bathed Adrienne's bare shoulders in a warm embrace, as she stepped through the curtained glass doors to the balcony. Needing a reprieve from the guests, and the ever-increasing flow of champagne, she sucked in a breath, filling her lungs as much as her corset would allow.

"Apologies for intruding," Monsieur Du Cormier's rasped voice startled her.

Adrienne composed herself, brushing her hands over her dress. "No intrusion, monsieur. I merely sought a breath of fresh air. The ballroom can get rather stifling during these big parties." Realizing she was rambling, Adrienne pressed her lips together, staring out across the darkened plantation.

"I agree. I found myself desiring the outdoors as well. I am afraid I am not used to these gatherings," he laughed low, coming up beside her.

"I can imagine they must seem rather daunting to someone unused to society." Adrienne bit her tongue. "Now I must apologize. My mouth has a mind of its own sometimes."

"No offense taken, mademoiselle. You are indeed correct in your observation. I am unused to society, as presented to me this evening. In fact, I think this starched collar makes it more unappealing."

Adrienne laughed unexpectedly, and Henri smiled, his first genuine one of the evening. "So, Mademoiselle Beaumont, what do you think of society?"

She rested her hands on the edge of the white balustrade. "I would much rather be sitting under that oak tree there with a book." She pointed a gloved finger to the shadowy tree, from which a swing swayed in the slight breeze.

Henri stepped closer, squinting into the darkness. "Ah, yes, seems quite pleasant."

"And you?" she probed, hungry for any information to help her decipher this man.

Clasping his hands behind his back, Henri rocked on his booted heels. "I prefer to ride through the fields, or hunt."

"I do believe we share the same passion for the outdoors, monsieur," Adrienne beamed, the moon setting off the sparks of gold in her hair.

"Indeed." The response came on an exhale of breath, as Henri felt something stir in his chest. "Should we return to the ballroom?" He held out his arm in a gentlemanly manner.

Adrienne inspected it carefully. "While I do

appreciate the kind gesture, Francine would cause me much...discomfort, should I accept. You are her betrothed."

The flash of something in her eyes did not go unnoticed, but Henri chose to ignore it, and deferred to Adrienne's wise counsel. He reckoned he had already narrowly avoided several outbursts during the evening thus far. "I shall leave you to your reflections then." Henri bowed, and disappeared through the doors.

Grasping the railing, Adrienne leaned over it slightly, gasping for breath. The encounter threw her guard completely off, leaving her feeling almost naked before the man. The sensation had her checking her dress, just in case some force had ripped it from her form. Being inexplicably drawn to a promised man, especially one promised to Francine, was completely, and utterly, unacceptable.

Resolved in her position not to pursue her curiosity, Adrienne composed herself, reentering the ballroom, only to be roughly yanked aside by Francine's cold hand.

"What were you doing out there with Monsieur Du Cormier?" Francine's hot breath scalded Adrienne's cheek.

Aghast at her sister's behavior, Adrienne delicately withdrew her arm from her grasp. "You are making a scene for nothing, Francine. I was merely taking some air, when he came upon me."

"He is mine. Do you understand?" The expression on Francine's face made her pretty, youthful features appear as ugly as an old hag.

"Perfectly. I want nothing to do with him."

Adrienne raced off, prior to her sister continuing her tirade. Her arm smarted from where Francine's nails grazed her skin.

Bessie, having witnessed the ordeal, hurried to her side. "What did that horrible witch do to you?" She gently inspected the half-moon marks, shaking her head in disgust. "George says the betrothal is all but finalized. Soon, she will be absorbed in planning the most extravagant wedding of the season, and you can be at peace." She caressed her friend's cheek.

Adrienne fought back tears. Francine had never made her cry previously, but maybe the tears were not for the abuse she had suffered. "You are right, Bessie. I do pity Monsieur Du Cormier, in a small way."

"Do not grow any sort of affection for him, for your sake, and his. You know I speak the truth, Addy." Bessie shook her head. She knew the mystery of Du Cormier would tempt Adrienne like no other.

Adrienne nodded. "Come. Let us have no more talk of betrothals and evil sisters. We shall enjoy the rest of the ball," she stated emphatically.

With an approving smile, Bessie and Adrienne let the atmosphere of the party take them away.

Spying Francine marching to Adrienne, Arnaud swiftly distracted Monsieur Du Cormier. "Henri, my good man, how are you enjoying the ball?"

Henri bowed solicitously. "It is a very lavish affair, Lord Beaumont. I am glad to have been invited."

"It's certainly our pleasure to host you. Have you given any thought to the matter we discussed the other week?" Arnaud inquired carefully, hoping and praying Francine had not put him off.

Henri's brow wrinkled. "You mean...ah, yes, Francine and the betrothal. If it is amenable, I would like to finalize everything immediately." His heart certainly wasn't into the match, but now he could ill afford to appear as a man who did not keep his word. "Actually, we can make the announcement tonight."

Arnaud clapped Henri on the back. "Excellent! Find Francine, and I will get the attention of the guests." He moved off to the center of the room.

Henri turned in time to see Adrienne retreating from Francine, whose expression made her appear like a witch from a fairy tale. He strode across the room, clearing his throat. "Francine, I have been speaking to your father..."

Suddenly, she was all smiles. "Oh! Monsieur Du Cormier! What about?"

Henri cleared his throat. "If you will have me, I should like to become your husband."

Francine fanned herself, feigning surprise. "Why, Monsieur...Henri...I would be honored!"

The timing was perfect, for at that moment, Arnaud drew the attention of the assembled guests. "Ladies and gentlemen, it is with my great pleasure that I announce the betrothal of Monsieur Henri Du Cormier to my daughter, Francine Beaumont. Shall we raise a glass to their health?"

Henri escorted Francine to the center of the room, and she lavished herself in the congratulations and good wishes. Arnaud clapped his hands. "A waltz for the new couple!"

The band struck up, and Francine faced her fiancé expectantly. Henri dutifully obliged, catching a glimpse of midnight blue out of the corner of his eye. As he spun Francine around, he managed to spy Adrienne, eyes lowered, face impassive. Prior to the dance's end, she vanished from the ballroom. He hoped his disappointment wasn't obvious to his betrothed, but she was again swept away in the congratulations of friends. The sensation he had made a horrible mistake crept its way into his head.

Adrienne fled the ballroom as the dance commenced, making her way to her bedroom. Her maid, Hetty, met her at the door. "Miss Adrienne! Is everything alright?"

Blinking several times, Adrienne turned the door handle, and entered her chamber. "Yes, Hetty. I suddenly did not feel well. I think this corset is laced too tightly, damn the fashion." She often spoke frankly in front of her maid, who was not shocked by the coarse language.

"Let's get you out of that dress, miss. I'm sure all you need is a good night's sleep." Hetty bustled around the room, laying out the cotton nightgown and robe for her mistress.

Adrienne stood patiently, waiting for Hetty to unlace the dress she had so long desired to wear for the evening. Now, it all seemed pointless. Her evening was inadvertently spoiled by Henri Du Cormier, his indecipherable gaze following her every movement. She knew enough to understand he desired her above her sister, but the deed was done. Francine and Henri would be married, and that would be the end of all of it.

"Miss?" Hetty motioned for Adrienne to step out of the dress, smoothing the ruffles gently, and laying it aside. Her nimble fingers unlaced the corset, and Adrienne finally felt like she could breathe. "I did try to keep it loose, Miss Adrienne."

Recognizing her tone may be cruel to the young maid, Adrienne softened. "Ignore me, Hetty. I find myself tired. You are right. I do need a good sleep."

After helping her mistress into her night clothes, Hetty dismissed herself, leaving Adrienne in the flickering candlelight. The party continued on, until the early hours of the morning, music drifting up to Adrienne's room. As hoof beats signaled carriages were being led to the front door, Adrienne brushed aside the lace curtains, and gazed down.

At that exact moment, fate dealt her a treacherous hand. Henri stared up at the house, his eyes burning into hers. She jumped back from the window, retreating to her bed, and drawing her knees up to her chest. She willed her heart to cease beating. Closing her eyes tightly, Adrienne desired nothing more than to drift into sleep, and never wake up.

4

Henri immediately doffed his coat upon entering the nearly vacant big house at St. Esprit. Many of the slaves would have retired for the evening, aside from his personal valet, Benjamin, or Benji for short. The statuesque man accepted his master's coat, only raising an eyebrow slightly at his odd behavior.

Since Master Henri bought St. Esprit, the slaves had given him a wide berth, unsure of the brooding man. Most feared the unknown, but Benji was no stranger to changing hands. He immediately offered his services, and found the man to be most cordial. Through this, Benji was able to allay the fears of the house slaves. However, the field workers still remained skeptical. Despite worry, nothing much had changed with the sale.

"May I get you a drink, Master Henri?" Benji

inquired, solicitously.

"No, thank you, Benji. You may retire for the evening. I will not require anything until midday. Can you tell the cook..." Henri faltered, trying to remember her name.

"Clotilde, Master Henri. Yes, I will relay the message." Benji had been brought up in big houses for his entire life. His language and manners were far above some of the other slaves, causing them to look upon him in a disdainful way. Benji merely considered it his duty to be amicable and subservient. He bowed his head, and retired.

Henri found his way into the dark study, a fire glowing low in the grate. The sun would rise soon, but in the meantime, he lit some candles. Neglected bookshelves lined the wall, but not a speck of dust would be found. Even though the former owner had preferred his cards to educational pursuits, the slaves had still kept the room spotless.

Wondering briefly as to the fate of the former owner, Henri banished it from his mind, determined not to dwell on the past. His dead uncle's money had bought him a place in high society, and a title would be forthcoming when Lord Beaumont passed. He sat in the plush armchair by the fire, jamming the poker into the coals, and stirring up the blaze. What would happen to Adrienne, when her father died?

Reclining back, he stretched his booted feet out to the warmth, even though the weather was more than pleasant at this time of year. Adrienne held for him all the mystery and beauty he could have ever desired in a partner. Cursing his impulsiveness, Henri could little complain. Fortune had treated him well to this point. Perhaps Francine was not as disagreeable as she seemed.

Chewing thoughtfully on his thumbnail, Henri contemplated the formation of a friendship with his future sister-in-law. In their brief conversations, he had discovered her wit. He knew she was well-read, poised, beautiful...probably a willing and generous lover... No! He could not allow his thoughts to drift to the impossible.

He moved to the desk with purpose, opening one of the locked drawers, and retrieving his journal, full of secrets and desires. Scrawling a missive across the page, he studied it, knowing he might later regret the damning words: *I love her. I will do anything to have her. I will kill for her*. He laughed at the foolish declaration, shoving the book back into his desk, and resolving nevermore to think of his sentiments.

Shoving himself out of the chair, Henri paced to the window, watching the sun rise over the trees. The slaves would be rising shortly to work the fields. The house would come to life, and he would be left alone again. St. Esprit needed the laughter of children, a woman's touch. Images of golden-haired children, running in the yard came to mind. He was surely damned. Grabbing a bottle of brandy from the liquor cabinet, Henri took himself upstairs to drown his sorrows, and secretly pray for intervention in his plight.

Ribbons trailing around her cheeks, Adrienne raced from the plantation house soon after rising. Her white lawn dress flitted around her legs, slippered feet slapping against the dirt path. None of the slaves were shocked by their mistress's appearance. Since childhood, Adrienne was proclaimed a free spirit, bound by nothing, and indulged in all things by her father. Slung over her arm was a wicker basket, containing two novels and some bread and cheese, bouncing against her side as she ran.

Finally, having placed some distance between herself and the house, Adrienne stopped, pulling an apple out of her pocket and biting into the crisp flesh. She hummed softly to herself, pausing to wave at some of the female slaves sweeping dirt off their porches. Out with Southern standards, her father was very generous with his slaves, scoffing whippings and harsh overseers.

A meandering creek traced the property line of the plantation. Adrienne knew St. Esprit was to the north, and Belle Rivière to the west, although they were not close in distance by any means. Settling herself down on the lush, green grass, Adrienne retrieved her book, opened it up to the marked page, and leaned against a tree.

"Interesting book?"

Adrienne scrambled to her feet, clutching a hand to her breast. "Monsieur Du Cormier, you really must stop startling me like this! My heart cannot take it." Her face burned red.

Henri stepped out from behind the tree. "Apologies again. I was taking a walk, and noticed you leaving the house." He gestured back to it. "I did not mean to intrude."

Retrieving her book, Adrienne searched for her basket, which had fallen over in her flight.

"You...you shouldn't sneak up on people unannounced."

"Again, I do apologize." Henri's hair was loose around his shoulders, giving him the appearance of a pirate plundering the seven seas. He lacked a jacket, his shirt open at the collar. "I assume the rest of the household is asleep?"

Keeping her eyes on him, Adrienne fumbled for the basket. "Er, yes, many of the guests left in the early hours of the morning." She replaced the contents. "I should return."

"Why did you leave the ball last night?" Henri circled her, bending down, and retrieving the second book. "*Charlotte Temple.* Hmm."

Adrienne raised an eyebrow, holding out her hand. "Yes."

He handed the book over. "And the reason for your departure?"

"I was unwell." She snatched the book, placing it back in her basket.

Henri stepped closer. "I do hope you are recovered."

"Much," she responded in a breathy whisper, feeling something building inside her.

"You should come see the library at St. Esprit. It is extensive."

"I should like that very much." Adrienne stepped back, needing to put some distance between herself and this overpowering man.

Squinting across the creek, Henri remarked, "Please tell your sister I should like to call on her this evening."

Adrienne turned, and fled, calling back over her shoulder. "I'm sure she will be most grateful!" She nearly tripped, but righted herself, returning to the plantation house with all speed.

Henri chuckled, watching her retreat. Spotting something fluttering in the grass, he knelt, retrieving one of the blue ribbons Adrienne had woven through her hair. Henri lifted it to his lips, rubbing the satin material between his calloused thumb and forefinger, before tucking it into his pocket. Whistling, he strolled back in the direction of his plantation.

Out of breath, Adrienne slammed the outside kitchen door, causing Helene to jump. "Lawdy, miss! What's chasin' you?" She tapped her wooden spoon against her hand. "Young ladies shouldn't run like that!"

Bringing a shaky hand to her hair, Adrienne let out a groan. "Oh no... he'll have it now..."

"What are you on about, miss?" Helene had her back turned to Adrienne again, stirring a pot on the stove.

Lamenting the loss of her ribbon, Adrienne mumbled, "Nothing, Helene. I better go see to Papa."

"I heard someone scratchin' around upstairs 'bout an hour ago, miss. You slow down, though. You'll make yourself sick! Can't have no sick youngins in this house!" Helene scolded, in her maternal way.

Adrienne's black mood melted away, and she gave the cook a kiss on the cheek. "I will, Helene. Thank you." She climbed the stairs, holding her hem up slightly. On the way to her father's study, she nearly walked headlong into Francine.

"Watch it, worm!" Francine sneered, taking in the rag-tag appearance of her sister. "Look at you! It will be a wonder if you win a husband, gallivanting around in dirty clothes."

Opening her mouth to tell Francine about her encounter with Henri, Adrienne thought better of it, and pressed her lips closed. "I shall endeavor to do better, sister."

"Good. We cannot have Henri thinking our family is a bunch of uncouth heathens. He's coming for dinner this evening." Francine pushed past Adrienne, and flounced into their father's study. Adrienne followed, keeping a safe distance.

"Ah, my girls. Did you sleep well?" Arnaud rose from behind his desk, bestowing a kiss on each of his children, drawing Adrienne further into the room.

Francine, irritated by the shift in attention, waved a paper missive in front of her father. "Monsieur Du Cormier is coming to dinner tonight, Father. He will want to finalize the betrothal; I am sure of it!"

"I thought it was already final?" Adrienne queried, tipping her head to the side.

Francine snorted. "Of course not, you ninny. Father must agree on a suitable dowry."

Adrienne turned from her sister, leaving her to plead with their father on that subject. She ran her finger across the spines of the novels lining her father's walls. Each one was a like a treasured friend, containing adventures of far off lands. She pictured her parents, fleeing from the persecution of the French Revolution. Their story was more than any of these authors could tell in a lifetime. If only she were lucky to have such a love.

"Adrienne! Are you listening?" Francine prodded her sister in the shoulder.

"Ompf! Yes?" Adrienne rubbed the offending spot.

Arnaud frowned. "Francine, you will treat your sister with more respect. Adrienne, would you be so kind as to loan Hetty to Francine for the evening? She wishes to try a new hairstyle."

Adrienne studied her sister carefully. "As long as she promises not to strike her. Last time, Hetty came back with a rather angry-looking red mark across her cheek."

"She pulled my hair. What was I supposed to do? Besides, she is a slave." Francine spun and left the room, ahead of any further admonishment from her father or sister.

Arnaud sighed, wrapping his youngest daughter in a hug. "She is difficult, but soon, it will pass, and we will be able to live in peace."

Adrienne rubbed her cheek against her father's bristled face. "I think Monsieur Du Cormier is much too good for her, Papa. He will have to put up with all her tantrums."

"I think he is up for the challenge. He does not strike me as a man who would back down easily."

Closing her eyes, Adrienne thought back to the warm laughter which caused her body to feel uncomfortably chilled. "I do hope you are right, Papa." Regret filled her traitorous heart.

5

“I am quite curious, Monsieur Du Cormier, as to the circumstances of your inherited wealth, and subsequent purchase of St. Esprit. There are rumors, you know, but I would like some of my fears allayed, before you marry Francine.” Arnaud offered his guest a cigar, having retired to his study for private discussion of matters deemed too indelicate for female ears.

Francine had soon vacated the parlor, loathed to sit with her younger sister, and Adrienne found herself kneeling outside her father’s study door, hoping for answers to her questions as well. She pressed her ear to the gold keyhole, straining to hear every piece of conversation.

“You are brave, Lord Beaumont. Most circumvent the question, fearing I am perhaps some dastardly thief, or villainous pirate.” Adrienne heard the flare of a match, and she knew both men would be enjoying the fruits of the plantation.

A chair squeaked, and her father's voice came once again. "Bravery has nothing to do with it, although I have faced much greater foes than the background of my future son-in-law." Mirth entered his tone, and Adrienne stifled a giggle.

"As I am sure many know, I bought St. Esprit from an unfortunate gambler, who whittled away his own fortune to pay his debts. The money came from a doting uncle, with no legitimate heirs. He passed away in England last year, and I was contacted by his solicitor here, being named as his only living relative. I traveled to England to complete the required paperwork, and prove my identity.

"When I came back, I spent some time in Virginia, working on the coast for a shipping company, resuming my normal life. However, one evening, I came across the doomed owner of my current home. He was in a serious situation, at risk of losing his home to debtors. I offered him a fair deal, tempted to try my hand at plantation ownership, and here I am. There is nothing illegal, or nefarious, about my business dealings, aside from my lack of birth."

Adrienne frowned. She had hoped there was much more to Henri's story than a fortuitous inheritance. Still, she speculated there may be something he was not telling her father.

Arnaud laughed. "You have been truly fortunate, my boy. I must admit, my own finances are not nearly as glorious as yours. We are barely keeping ourselves afloat here."

"I understand that from speaking to some of your neighbors, Lord Beaumont. I apologize for prying."

"When my wife passed, I was devastated. I loved my Marie dearly, and I neglected the plantation sorely. We lost many slaves, to pay debts accrued during this time. I am getting back on my feet, but I fear we will continue to manage." Her father rose, pacing the room. She could hear his boots scraping on the floor. "I am afraid I have little to offer by way of dowry for Francine, aside from the promise of a title upon my death, and the inheritance of this plantation."

"What about Adrienne? What will happen to her?"

Adrienne bit her knuckle. How dare he worry about her well-being? Surely it was no concern of his! Still, his consideration was flattering.

"I am hoping Adrienne will find a kind gentleman to marry. She is a free spirit, but a prize to any man in the state!"

"To be sure," Henri murmured.

Arnaud sighed. "Were she the eldest...she has a good head for business, and would run the plantation well, were it appropriate."

The compliment had Adrienne puffing up with pride. She had sat at her father's knee, observing and absorbing all the information she could from a young age.

"Early summer would be suitable, if you were amenable to the idea." The conversation had moved on to discussion of a wedding date.

"If that is enough time to prepare. I do want to offer to help with the costs of the wedding." Arnaud began to protest, but Henri stopped him. "Please, I insist. Save some of your money for Adrienne, when her time comes."

Footsteps approached the door, and Adrienne scrambled to her feet, searching frantically for a place to hide. She secreted herself behind one of the velvet drapes at the end of the hall, praying no one would see her when the study door swung open. Both men were distracted by conversation, and retreated in the opposite direction. Sighing with relief, Adrienne stepped from behind the curtain, only to come face-to-face with the one person she wished to avoid.

"You really are a clever little spy. I do think many foreign forces would love putting your tactics to good use," Henri joked, smiling down at her.

Adrienne brushed past him. "I haven't any idea what you are talking about."

His laughter met her ears, and she stopped, spinning to face him. "I would like my ribbon back!"

Henri feigned confusion. "What ribbon?"

"The one you *stole* this morning!"

Bowing low, Henri lifted his head. "I do hate to disappoint, my lady, but I do not have the offending item."

Adrienne clenched her fists, mouth opening and closing in outrage. She stamped her slippered foot, and moved away, restraining herself from running as fast as she could.

Henri shook his head in amusement, returning to the study to retrieve his frock coat. As he departed, he ran into someone he heartily wished to avoid. Francine emerged from another room, missing her sister. Henri secretly thanked God, as he was sure the almost-encounter would have caused later hardship for Adrienne.

"Monsieur." Francine dipped into a curtsey. "I wished to bid you farewell, before you left."

Henri inclined his head. "Thank you, mademoiselle. It has been a pleasant evening. I look forward to many more."

Francine linked her arm through his, traversing the hallway towards the front entryway. "I thought I would like to see your St. Esprit, before we are married. Is that agreeable?"

"You and your family would do me a great honor of visiting tomorrow evening for dinner."

Her face tightened, and Henri could tell she had been hoping the invitation would only extend to her. He quickly tried to remedy his fault. "Certainly your family would want to know you will be safe in my care. There will be time for us to be alone later." Henri felt a pull in his stomach, lamenting the lie.

Francine's face drained of all hate. "Yes, Henri. Thank you for the consideration to my father and sister." She tilted her face up, expectantly, once they reached the door, closing her eyes delicately.

Henri shifted his gaze around the foyer, knowing he had little time to make a decision. He placed a chaste kiss on Francine's thin lips. "Until tomorrow, my dear." He added the endearment, against his better judgment.

Placated for the time being, Francine ushered him out. "I look forward to it." As soon as the door closed, she vented her frustration on a china vase of flowers. "Damn all men!"

One of the house slaves whimpered, having entered the room at the wrong moment. A fresh gash formed on her cheek, as a piece of porcelain sliced her skin.

"Don't just stand there, girl! Clean this up!" Francine stomped up the stairs, grinding her foot into the petals, and leaving the hapless woman to carefully dispose of the jagged remains, and massacred flowers.

Francine's mood darkened the entire household the following day, despite her secret joy at the pending visit. She wanted to retain her control over this household until she moved on to St. Esprit. Henri's kiss the previous night had left her blood running cold. There had been no warmth behind his voice, or his actions, and she knew it. He did not love her, nor would he ever. For this, she would make every moment of their marriage hell.

A house slave, serving the breakfast, earned a fierce slap at Francine's hand for serving cold food. She ignored her younger sister's gasp, sneering horribly. "We are their mistresses, Adrienne. They expect this. After all, they are filthy creatures. Their only lot in life is to serve us."

Arnaud hit his fist on the table, barking out, "You will not speak that way while you are under my roof. I only hope you treat your future husband's home with more respect."

"He will do what I say, or there will be consequences." Francine left the table, slamming the door behind her.

Adrienne shuddered, rubbing her arms. She rose, and went to check on Sybil, the maid who had been struck. She was cowering in the corner. "Please, are you hurt?" Her gentle tone lulled the slave out of her fetal position. It was then Adrienne spied the freshly opened cut. "Go to Helene. Tell her to tend your wound. We will be fine here," she assured. Bobbing a curtsey, Sybil raced from the room.

Arnaud rubbed the back of his neck, trying to ease the tension. "Adrienne, I would like to task you with something very important. My final wishes have been made plain to your sister's betrothed. Upon my death, the plantation will go to Francine. I know it is not ideal, but it is expected. However, I need you to make sure the slaves are issued with their freedom papers, the instant you learn of my death."

Rushing around to her father's side, Adrienne grasped his hand. "I do not like to hear you speak such words, Papa, but I will make sure everything is as it should be."

"Good. I received word this morning, which Francine has conveniently forgotten it seems, that we have been invited to St. Esprit this evening for dinner. As much as she would loathe us to go, we have a duty." Arnaud patted his daughter's hand.

Adrienne remained silent, her desire to see the impenetrable St. Esprit. Everyone in the society knew about the previous owner, who had never made any effort to integrate into their circles. Henri's earlier comment about the library played on her mind as well.

"Adrienne?" Arnaud's worried tone entered her thoughts.

"Yes, Papa, we do have a duty," Adrienne hurried

to allay his fears. "I believe I have a headache, and would like to lay down to be fresh for the evening."

"Very well, *ma petite*. I will need you by my side tonight, so rest well. I will send Hetty with a cool compress for your head." Arnaud was distracted, staring out the window at the overseer on horseback. "I will be in my study, should you require anything." He stood, placing a kiss on her brow, and guided her from the room.

Adrienne climbed the stairs, listening carefully for signs of her sister. As usual, Francine had ensconced herself in her room, and Adrienne reached her own chamber in peace. Leaning against her closed door, she stared forlornly at the pocket portrait of her mother, balanced on her vanity.

"Mama, I wish you were here. You could soothe my troubles."

A gentle knock came from the portal. "Miss Adrienne? Helene said you would be needin' a compress. May I come in?"

Adrienne stepped forward, and opened the door. "Yes, thank you...Hetty! What happened?"

Hetty's blackened eye shone out against her creamy brown skin. "Oh, miss, it's truly nothing. My own carelessness."

Adrienne pulled her into the room, shutting the door firmly. "Hetty, do not lie to me! Francine did this, am I right?"

Turning her eyes down to the floor, Hetty held the basin with the cloth tightly. "I dare not say, Miss Adrienne. Please, don't make me!"

Adrienne's anger rose, a rare emotion in the normally placid and kind woman. "I will not stand for it, Hetty."

"Many more slaves than I get worse, and then some. You and Master Arnaud are kind, so it's worth one woman's rage," Hetty confessed hurriedly. She placed the basin on the table by the bed. "If you will excuse me, miss, I have to look out your gown and get it ready for tonight."

"The pale blue, please, Hetty. Thank you." Adrienne peered kindly at the young girl. "Do not worry either, Hetty. One day, all will come to right."

Hetty curtseyed carefully, and left the room. Adrienne moved to the bed, sitting on the edge of the quilt. Francine would abuse the slaves at St. Esprit terribly. She wondered if Henri would stand for the behavior, although she was sure Francine would merely take her beatings to private settings. Sighing deeply, Adrienne withdrew her book from under her pillow, letting herself be swept away in the story, trying to forget her worries for the moment.

6

"It is certainly in need of repair." Francine turned up her nose as the carriage passed some fallen slave quarters.

"I imagine the previous owner had little care for the conditions his slaves lived in," Arnaud remarked. "But Monsieur Du Cormier seems to be managing well." He gestured to some of the new quarters being built by the ramshackle ones.

Adrienne kept her thoughts to herself, watching as the slaves worked. The carriage circled the front drive, coming to a stop in front of the main house. There were several large trees, the branches almost shielding the building from view. Henri stood on the porch, eyes impassive as he watched the carriage. Moving to Francine's side, he held out his hand.

"Mademoiselle."

Francine delicately placed her hand into his,

leaving her father and sister to be assisted by others, even though Henri appeared to want to do it himself. Instead, he led the small party into the front foyer. “Welcome to my home. I do hope you’ll find it to your satisfaction.”

Adrienne gazed around at the dimly lit entry, taking in some grim portraits on the walls. The only bright spot of the room was a vase of fresh flowers. “Who are they?” she piped up, gesturing to the paintings.

Henri smiled warmly at her. “I honestly have no idea. I bought the house as is. I will leave decorating to my future wife.” He placed a hand over Francine’s.

Adrienne’s stomach twisted into a firm knot. “I should like to see the rest of the home, wouldn’t you, Francine?” Shifting the attention to her sister was the best tactic.

Narrowing her eyes, Francine peered haughtily around. “I do suppose it could have some redeeming qualities, if one looks for them. Yes, Henri, please show us the rest of your...our home.” She flashed a forced smile.

Arnaud and Henri spoke frankly about the prospects of the plantation as they toured the lower floor. Francine delicately muffled a yawn. Business dealings were of no interest to her. Adrienne trailed along behind. As the party advanced, Adrienne caught movement from the corner of her eye. Glancing ahead, she made sure no one was watching as she investigated.

A young slave girl, maybe twelve, peered out from behind one of the curtains. Her expressive, dark eyes told of a much older soul inhabiting the slight body. She wore a colorful, striped skirt and simple cream blouse, her hair hidden beneath an earthen colored scarf.

"Hello," Adrienne murmured, approaching slowly. "What is your name?"

Slender fingers clasped together, her eyes flitting away. "Sabine, miss."

Smiling warmly, Adrienne tried to allay the child's fears. "Hello, Sabine. My name is Adrienne."

Sabine gave a jerking curtsey. "You are a kind lady, miss. The *loa* are wary of your sister though." She lifted a hand, pointing at Francine's retreating back.

Swiveling, Adrienne noticed they were now alone in the corridor. Tilting her head to the side, she inquired further of the girl. "Who are the *loa*?"

"I shouldn't trouble the miss with it. My mother says it's not for all ears." Her eyes widened, and fear caused her pupils to dilate.

Curiosity overwhelmed Adrienne, and she pressed further. "Please, Sabine. I am fascinated by all things."

"Since they say you are trustworthy, I will tell you. The *loa* serve Bondye. We honor them in our dances. They are demanding, but will listen to requests." She gestured for Adrienne to come closer, her sweet voice filling her ear. "Mama says we have to respect them, or they will bring down certain death on us all."

"And where is your mother?" Adrienne felt a cool breeze down her neck, and she shuddered.

Sabine smiled, showing off straight, white teeth. "She is in the kitchens, miss. Mama is Master Henri's cook. She says the *loa* like Master Henri.

The old master was brutal to us."

"You use very good language, Sabine. Who taught you?" Rubbing away the persistent chill, Adrienne had a strong desire to continue to speak of less foreboding topics.

"The old mistress. She was a beautiful lady, miss. When she died, Master went into a deep melancholy. He drowned his sorrows in drink and gambling. When Master Henri bought the plantation, Master put a bullet in his head."

Adrienne gasped, holding a hand to her throat, and Sabine continued, "Master Henri was left the money he would have spent on the plantation, but no one knows that, miss. He paid the old Master's debts, and for his funeral."

"Adrienne?" Arnaud's voice echoed from a nearby room. "You may like to see this. Where are you?"

Adrienne turned to call back, "I'm here. Coming. Thank you, Sa..." But when she looked back, the girl had vanished. Picking up her skirts, Adrienne raced towards her father's voice, heart pounding in fear. The trio took in her panicked expression.

"Why, Adrienne, are you well, *ma petite*?" Arnaud clutched his daughter's shoulders, as she paled.

Pressing a hand to her brow, Adrienne nodded, and forced a laugh. "Yes, Papa. Something gave me a fright, that's all."

Henri shook his head. "The house slaves refuse to touch the west wing. They say the old mistress haunts the rooms."

Francine giggled, placing her fingers over her mouth. "Adrienne, it's all that reading you do. It's simply rattled your head!" She endeavored to draw Henri's attention back to her with a squeeze of his arm, but he was too distracted waiting for her younger sister's reaction.

Adrienne momentarily forgot the encounter when she saw the room. Sucking in a breath, her eyes skimmed row after row of books. She hesitantly reached out, tracing a fingertip over the spine of one novel, moving along the shelf. "This is a remarkable collection, Monsieur Du Cormier."

Henri shrugged, trying not to seem too pleased by her reaction. He wished he could make the other two in their party disappear for a few moments, so he might enjoy Adrienne privately. "Ah, yes, it seems the old owner thought numerous books would make him appear more knowledgeable. Little good that did him."

Francine tittered. "Oh, Henri, you are so funny!"

"Come. I believe dinner will be served shortly." Henri guided Francine and Arnaud from the room.

Adrienne shot a longing gaze at the books, wanting to stay longer. Her mouth opened to voice her desires, but she found herself alone again. The curtains billowed out from the window, as an evening breeze entered the deserted library. Shuddering again, Adrienne encompassed her body with her arms, glancing warily around, expecting to see Sabine appear again. When the silence threatened to overwhelm her, Adrienne briskly walked from the room, catching the swishing of Francine's skirts as they turned into the dining room.

“Marvelous meal, Du Cormier! I must commend you on your cook. Truly, you inherited a gem in that woman!” Arnaud patted his stomach approvingly, his waistcoat threatening to burst a button.

Henri swirled the red wine in his glass, leaning back in his chair. “Clotilde certainly keeps me well fed.”

Francine gestured to a house slave to refill her glass. The tour of her future residence was tedious. The décor was in desperate need of style. Once she lived here, things would most certainly change. Francine shook her glass impatiently, as the house slave slowly approached her. *The impertinence of the slaves will be remedied as well,* she thought with bitter malice. The man carefully tipped more wine out of a decanter. He startled, making eye contact with Adrienne across the table. A drop of red blossomed on the pure white tablecloth.

“Clumsy fool!” The words slipped unrestrained from Francine’s lips.

Henri lifted an eyebrow in disapproval, waving his hand to dismiss the slave. “It was an accident, my dear. Surely no damage was truly done.”

Scoffing, Francine veiled her displeasure, scrutinizing her sister, and wondering what had distracted the slave. She swirled her tongue around the rich wine. These sorts of delicacies were certainly worth sacrificing herself to the man who admonished her so readily. “Why, yes, where are my manners? It surely was an accident.” She beamed at the slave with a villainous grin which evaded her eyes. “Be more careful next time, won’t you?”

“Yes, miss. I’s sorry.” The man lowered his eyes.

Pleased at the difference displayed by the slave to her, Francine spun her head around again to peer at Adrienne. She averted her gaze, playing with the corner of a cloth napkin, her mind in another universe. “Adrienne, did you enjoy the tour?”

Adrienne’s head snapped up. “Yes, it was lovely, especially the library.”

“You will come visit me when I am married, won’t you?” She did her best to slip honey into her tone, but those who knew her best would see through the façade.

“If you wish me to, sister,” Adrienne murmured, and went back to fidgeting.

Francine’s ire rose to a point, where she soon would not be able to contain her biting remarks. Her mouth gaped to shoot some barb at her sister, when a loud rumble of thunder filled the room, followed by a crack of lightning. “Oh my!” If there was something Francine despised, despite her bravado, it was thunderstorms. “Papa!”

Henri placed his glass down, and strode to the window, peeling back the curtain. “Ah, looks as though we are in for a hearty spring storm. I can accommodate you here tonight, if you wish?” He directed the question to Arnaud.

“Ah, yes, that would be most gracious of you. I will have a slave go back for our things.”

“Nonsense. We have plenty of clothing here. It seemed the previous mistress kept many fine dresses. I am sure your daughters will have little trouble finding something to wear for the night.” Henri rubbed his chin in contemplation. “I never had cause to look through those wardrobes. Huh."

Francine balked at the suggestion she wear some dead woman's clothing, but she realized this would be an excellent opportunity to bind Henri to her completely. For once, a thunderstorm had brought good fortune. "What a brilliant idea. Adrienne, shall we go find something suitable?"

Adrienne stood with some reluctance. "Yes, I think that would..."

"Excellent. Come along, Addy." She held out her hand in mock sisterly affection.

Hesitantly, Adrienne moved along after her. Once out in the hall, Francine snatched her hand away. "Wearing some dead woman's clothing? How dare he suggest that?" she ranted, following a house slave holding a lamp, little care for her free-flowing words.

"Francine, he was just being polite..." Adrienne's words fell on deaf ears.

"Ha! Polite? I swear, one of the first things I will do when I move here, is burn all her clothing in the yard!"

"She never did anything to you, though. You would dishonor her memory?" Aghast, her younger sister stopped suddenly.

"By the time I am through here, everyone will say my name with reverence." Francine tossed her skirts to the side. "Move! I want this repulsive experience over with, as soon as possible!"

7

Lightning lit up the bedroom where Adrienne sought rest. She tossed and turned on the comfortable mattress, unable to find respite from her troubling thoughts. Pinprick bumps rose on her arms, even though the room was warmed by a crackling fire. Wrapping the quilt tightly around her body, Adrienne watched the shadows dance on the wall.

As moments passed, Adrienne's eyelids grew heavy, and sleep would be imminent. The whoosh of the curtains flying open, and the rain rattling against the sill, drew her upright in bed, blonde curls cascading around her shoulders. She leapt up, and snatched a shawl from the end of the bed, making haste to the window to stop the water from getting in.

Her heart beat a tattoo in her ribcage, as she

desperately struggled with the old, wooden shutters. “How odd.” She attempted to soothe her own shattered nerves, rubbing a hand over the window, and looking out. People were running from the house to a barn in the distance; a ghostly silhouette against the backdrop of the storm.

Adrienne stepped back, her intention to seek the sanctuary of her bed, but her mind refused to cease. Placing her slippers on, she wrapped the shawl tighter around her form, resolved in finding out what was going on. She crept down the stairs, listening for any signs of movement in the house. Hearing none, she continued on her mission.

The front door was wide open. Adrienne glanced furtively over her shoulder, hoping to see someone standing there, but there was no one. She stepped over the threshold, moving out onto the porch.

“Miss? What are you doing?” Sabine’s haunting eyes reflected a bolt of lightning streaking across the sky. She stepped from the darkness, covered in a black cloak.

Adrienne felt her nerves slipping. “I heard a noise, and I came down to investigate. Why are you outside in the storm?”

She pointed a finger silently towards the barn. “My mother is holding a ceremony.”

Struggling to find words, Adrienne inhaled. “What sort of ceremony?”

“She’s a priestess,” Sabine moved closer. “When I am grown, I will be one as well.”

Against her better judgment, Adrienne held out her hand. “Can you show me?” Sabine hesitated for only a moment, dragging her out into the tempestuous night.

Unable to sleep, Henri was down in his study, something having drawn him to the window. Frowning, Henri watched as a white-gowned wraith was being pulled after a small, cloaked figure. He shook his head a few times, wondering if the storm was playing tricks on his eyes. It was then he realized the gowned one was Adrienne. Placing down his glass of whiskey, Henri hurried from the room, finding the same open front door.

"Strange." Stepping out into the waning storm, he pulled the portal closed behind him, following the same path as the pair.

They withdrew from the drizzling weather, into a barn. Henri instantly regretted not bringing along some sort of weapon, in case he encountered a threat. Circling around the back, he leaned against the wooden structure, pushing his wet hair out of his eyes. He could hear singing, gradually rising to a fevered pitch. Feet stomped the ground, and hands clapped to an unknown rhythm. Deciding he had to see the cause of the ruckus, he found an opening in the wood, and pressed his face to the crack.

Henri couldn't see Adrienne immediately, but he did see Clotilde. She was dressed in a manner he had never seen before, colorful scarves draping her head, and a full, striped skirt. Her hands were outstretched, chin tilted to the sky. French poured from her lips, and Henri roughly translated the words in his head. She was calling on a spirit, a *loa*. He knew instantly he was witnessing a voodoo ceremony.

A man in one of the taverns in New Orleans had warned him the slaves were particularly superstitious in Louisiana. Henri had brushed off the notion, carrying the revolutionary idea that slaves could practice what they wished, as long as it did not interfere with their work.

"You don't know what you're saying, boy. They'll curse you as soon as bless ya!" The old timer had croaked, shaking a gnarled finger at Henri.

Henri had shaken his head, indulging in another drink. "You're stuck too much in the past."

"They did it in Haiti! What makes you think it won't happen here?"

Vaguely remembering the talk of rebellion thirty years' prior, Henri had been a twinkle in his father's eye at the time. People still worried about the uprising, where some five thousand white people had been brutally massacred. Many had fled to Louisiana, so Henri hadn't been surprised by the old man's antiquated fears.

"Surely the slaves there were less civil than the ones here. Look, if it makes them happy, why should I interfere?"

Now he was watching one of the very rituals many plantation owners had banned, and brutally punished. A whirl of white caught his eye, and he saw Adrienne kneeling in a stall with Sabine, Clotilde's daughter.

"We have a dark presence in our home!" Clotilde's normally passive and soft voice took on an authoritative tone. Those gathered responded in kind, and the singing intensified. "We have had many a dark cloud come over our home. Master Black lost his way to greed. Master Henri is good and kind. We are lucky." Agreement echoed in the barn walls. "But she threatens to return." Moans filled the room, people keeled over, clutching their heads as if in pain.

She? The old mistress? No, it cannot be. By all accounts, she was a kind, generous woman. Henri's confusion deepened.

"We did not appease the Guédé, Priestess!"

Clotilde hushed the woman who had cried out. "We must not speak their name. The Baron has his purposes. We are being given another chance to rid the living world of her."

"We watched him put her in the ground. That's enough!" Benji stepped forward, holding out his hands in supplication. "There are many evil white people in the world."

Henri restrained himself from calling out to ask who they were talking about. They trusted him, and if he disturbed their ceremony, the trust might fade.

"It makes no matter, Benji. If the Baron refused to let her pass, she would seek vengeance," Clotilde continued on. "She forced us to use the arts for her will. This one will, too. We must convene in a week, at the rise of the full moon, and make offerings. He will help us."

The group dispersed, walking out into the cool night. The storm had passed, but the branches of the surrounding trees still dripped heavy drops from their leaning branches. Henri waited, knowing Adrienne would as well, to make sure she wasn't seen. Skirting the side of the barn, he caught them both by the arm the moment they exited. Sabine screamed.

"Hush! I'm not going to hurt you, Sabine." Henri

tried to soothe the panicking girl.

Adrienne, angered at his intrusion, yanked her arm from his grasp. "What are you doing here?"

"I could ask you the same question! Tell me why you are here." He towered over her as they stood toe to toe.

Placing a gentle hand on Sabine's shoulder, Adrienne turned away from Henri. "Sabine, you are fine. Monsieur Du Cormier will not cause you harm or trouble. Go back to the house, and your mother. Speak of this to no one." With an encouraging smile, Sabine's fears drained away, and she scampered off towards the kitchens.

Henri ground his teeth together, not in anger, but in disappointment. Adrienne's kind manner did not go unnoticed. Instantly, she had gained the trust of the skittish daughter of the cook. Still, despite his admiration, young women should not go running off to observe voodoo ceremonies. "I did ask you a question, mademoiselle."

Aware of her lack of proper clothing, Adrienne tucked the shawl around herself. "No, you demanded to know my purpose here. It is none of your concern, as I do not answer to you."

"Everything about you concerns me!" he shouted, recognizing the admission may drive her further from him.

"Why should it?" Her gorgeous eyes narrowed, facing him once again. "You are to marry my sister, a pact that should not be broken, even if you fancy yourself infatuated."

Henri's pride took a drastic hit with her admonishment. She was no fool, seeing through him almost instantly. "And if I do fancy myself infatuated, what then?" His voice deepened, and the urge to reach out and touch her pulled at his heart.

Adrienne faltered. "You push it back. It is impossible to act on it." She glanced over at the house, planning her flight.

"Damn to social convention!" Henri regained her attention rapidly, shock passing over her rosy cheeks. She colored at his outburst.

"I am going back to the house. The evening air is chilly, and I do not wish to burden you with my presence, should I grow ill." Adrienne departed his company, without waiting for an answer.

Henri contemplated calling her back, but he knew she would refuse. He cursed himself for speaking too freely. She must be conflicted by his frank admission, knowing he was betrothed to her sister. Perhaps he was jumping ahead of himself. Could Adrienne carry the same blazing torch for him, that he tendered for her?

Walking into the barn, he carefully put out the remaining lanterns forgotten in the haste of the party to depart. Leaving them burning would be dangerous. Leaving many things burning would prove dangerous. Walking out into the rain fresh air, Henri inhaled deeply. He rubbed the bridge of his nose, and banished all thought of Adrienne for the moment. His sole focus had to be, needed to be, Francine, despite what he yearned for in his heart.

Fists clenched on the curtains, Francine watched as first Adrienne, then Henri came back to the house. Her rage nearly had her confronting the pair immediately. How dare he traipse out into the storm after her sister when she was more than willing to offer him her body? Her earlier search for her betrothed had proved futile, and now, she knew why. He yearned for her younger sister.

Letting out a muted grunt of anger, Francine yanked the offending curtains closed. How dare they show her something she did not want to recognize? All the looks and attention to Adrienne made sense. She must be punished for enticing him in such a manner. Crossing her arms, she paced across the room. Maybe Adrienne had spurned his advances.

"Why should she have the right to spurn anyone, when I was never given the chance?" Francine whispered in the darkness, feeling somewhat sorry for her situation. She refused to listen the small voice in the back of her head, saying Adrienne was blameless.

"Blameless? Ha! She has always been the favorite, even when Mother was alive. I may not like that I am marrying Henri Du Cormier, but I will be damned to see anyone else take him from me. Oh yes, he will suffer at my hands, there is little doubt!" Satisfied with her final proclamation, Francine returned to bed.

Sabine stifled a cry. Her mother was right. Evil had returned to the house. Slipping away from the future mistress's door, she fled down a back passage, determined to make the woman pay for the curse she would bring down upon St. Esprit.

8

Adrienne heard both men speaking, before entering the dining room. Her memory trickled back to the previous night, and the voodoo ceremony she had witnessed. Although nothing of great note had taken place, she now had a strong desire to see the ceremony where they claimed they would banish evil from the home. Sabine was adamant Francine bore a vengeful spirit inside her, in the form of a previous mistress of the plantation.

"When Mama was young, there was a horrible woman. She was Master Black's mother. Her mind and body were cruel. She often asked Grandmère to invoke the *loa* for horrible purposes. Slaves died in her madness, Mama said." All was whispered in Adrienne's ear, as they crouched unseen in the barn. "When she died, Grandmère invoked the Baron to keep her spirit from crossing over. No one knew this, except Mama. Mama knew, though, the Baron could only be appeased for so long, before becoming greedy, as is his way…"

Voodoo certainly was a superstitious religion, Adrienne concluded, crossing into the room, as the smells of rich foods tempted her stomach.

"Ah, good morning, *ma petite*. Did you sleep well?" Arnaud rose from the table, bestowing a kiss on his daughter's cheek.

Adrienne sat down, placing her napkin delicately over her lap. "I did, Papa, thank you kindly."

"The storm did not disturb you, I trust?"

Meeting Henri's smoldering gaze, Adrienne pertly responded, "No, I was not disturbed in the least."

His lips turned up in a half smile, giving him a very roguish appearance. "Excellent."

As Adrienne waited to be served, she had a mind to play this game with Henri. "Do you find storms disturb your sleep, sir?"

"Not in the least. I weathered many a storm on the Atlantic traveling to England. I find them invigorating, to say the least." His gray eyes never left hers.

Pausing in their banter, to allow Adrienne's plate to be placed before her, there were no further opportunities to discuss the topic of storms. Francine came into the room, a smile plastered on her strained features.

"Good morning, Francine. Did the storm disturb your sleep?" Arnaud questioned, taking no notice of the tense look between Adrienne and Henri.

"Not at all. I am not a babe any longer, Father. Storms do not bother me," she lied prettily, seating herself next to Henri. “I should like to tour the grounds today, Henri, if you would care to show me. I am sure my father and sister would like to get home.”

Arnaud cleared his throat. “Without an escort? That is highly improper, Francine.”

“I hardly think it’s improper to see my future home, do you?” There was no convincing her either way.

Henri cleared his throat. “For propriety’s sake, maybe your sister could stay, and your father can go back to the plantation?” The solution seemed logical to him, but Adrienne immediately balked at the idea, stiffening visibly in her chair.

Again, her father paid little notice to his youngest daughter’s discomfort. “Yes, an excellent idea! I have business to attend to back at the plantation anyway. Are you amenable to the idea, Adrienne?”

She was hardly amenable to spending a day at Francine’s whim. The thought immediately resulted in a throbbing headache at her temples. Still, she smiled, knowing it would please her father. “If you wish, Papa. I should like to see the rest of the plantation.”

“It’s settled then. I shall call round for your coach, Lord Beaumont.” Henri laid firm the plans, before any further objection could be made.

“We will see you off, Papa,” Francine interjected, her cheeks burning red at the audacity of Henri’s proposal.

“Lovely, my dears. I do hope you enjoy your day.” Arnaud stood, discretely placing a hand on his stomach, to staunch the ulcerous pain.

Adrienne went to her father, looping an arm through his to escort him out onto the wraparound porch. As they exited into the rain-freshened air, she studied him carefully. "Will you be well on your own, Papa?"

"Of course, *ma petite*. I have Helene to fret over me, no? You must enjoy your tour of the plantation grounds." In a lowered tone, he added, "And make sure Francine keeps her temper."

Placing a kiss on her father's cheek, Adrienne assured him she would obey his request. She gazed up at their coachman, issuing a final request. "Please tell Helene to put Lord Beaumont to bed upon his return. I fear he is not well." The man tipped his hat, and the coach disappeared down the winding path.

Francine desperately wanted to confront her sister about the previous evening, and as she watched their father depart, she had the perfect opportunity. She stepped off the porch, swiftly crossing to her sister. Henri had turned to the side to deal with a matter with the overseer, so she knew she would not be interrupted.

"Why was Father so eager for you to stay?" Francine wound her fingers around Adrienne's forearm tightly.

Adrienne winced as her sister's nails dug into her flesh. "I am sure he merely wanted to make sure all propriety was kept, seeing as this is to be a very favorable match."

"Propriety indeed, sister. I saw you last night with Henri." Francine watched with hidden glee, as Adrienne's cheeks paled.

"Last night? I think you may be mistaken..."

Francine elicited a yelp from Adrienne, as her arm was tugged. "Do not lie to me! I saw you, along with that little slave bitch. Hear me now, sister. I maintain no qualms about having her whipped within an inch of her life, should I find you were alone with Henri again. He is mine, and I have great plans for this dump."

"Francine? What on Earth are you doing to Adrienne?" Henri strode across the yard towards them.

Francine dropped her hand immediately. "She was shaky, sir. Our father's health grieves her greatly."

"Mademoiselle, you must take me for a fool." He moved towards Adrienne, inspecting her bruised skin. "Hmm, you held her too tightly. Hear me now. I will not accept violence of any kind here, not to your family, nor to the slaves. Do you understand?"

Being scolded in such a manner had Francine grinding her back teeth together in pure rage. She met Henri's eyes with malice. "You should not presume to tell me how to behave, *sir*. I can ruin you in an instant." She flounced back towards the house. "I shall be in the parlor, until such a time as the tour is deemed concluded. I do not want to traipse about in mud, and ruin my skirts!"

The door slammed, echoing through the yard. Heads turned to see the source of the sound, before people went back about their business. Henri took a tentative step towards the house, but stopped, lowering his head.

"I have made a terrible mistake, Adrienne, and now I must pay for it."

Trembling at the attack launched by her sister,

she was unsure how to comfort her future brother-in-law. She knew she must think of him as nothing more, from that point. "It has happened many times in our youth. You should not let her trouble you. Mayhap marriage will bring about change in her." Adrienne attempted to be optimistic, but felt in her heart, there was nothing to sate the beast.

Shaking his head, Henri did not reply. He moved away, going to seek out his disgruntled fiancée, and try to allay her misguided thoughts. It was the proper thing to do, despite his desire to throw caution to the wind. Leaving Adrienne rubbing her arms in the yard, he headed in the direction of the parlor, once dominated by the late master's mother.

Francine sat primly in one of the lavishly upholstered chairs. "Henri, darling, please forgive my outburst. It was most unacceptable."

Her change in demeanor struck him as peculiar. "You seemed very distressed. Do you care to enlighten me as to what has caused this?"

"I thought, in my sleep disturbed state, I saw you and my sister last night in the storm." Her eyes narrowed.

Henri knew he must confess, if there was to be any temporary tranquility in his home. "Yes, my dearest, you did see me out by the barn."

Francine's mouth dropped open in indignation, but Henri knelt by her side. "You see, I, too, could not sleep because of the storm. I saw Adrienne leave the house with Sabine, the daughter of my cook. Fearing there was some mischief afoot, I followed them to ensure their safety."

How noble, Francine thought bitingly. "And was my sister well, or was the girl misleading her?"

Henri rocked back on his heels. “I suppose since you are to be mistress of my home, you should know, some of the slaves practice old rites, brought over from Haiti.”

“Voodoo? Yes, murmurs of the barbaric practice have been discussed in our circles. Was Adrienne attending such a ritual?” Her lips twisted, formulating a plan to take advantage of this superstitious belief system, as soon as humanly possible.

“Yes. Curiosity got the better of your sister. I am pleased to say she returned to the home unscathed, and I have warned Sabine to be more cautious in the future, with who she invites to these rituals.” Standing, Henri crossed the rug to the window, staring out at the barn. He locked his hands behind his back. “I should wish the matter closed. Your father asked me to watch out for Adrienne, especially in his weakened state. I take that charge seriously, mademoiselle. Please do not doubt my honor.”

“As you wish, Henri,” Francine purred demurely. “I should wish our families to be content together.”

A twinge irritated the back of Henri’s neck, and he rubbed it absently. “Yes, thank you. Now, it would please me greatly to escort you around the grounds of your future home. We might take a carriage, so you will not damage your lovely skirts.”

“And Adrienne?”

Henri turned, and cleared his throat. “I will ask her to stay behind in the library. Will this satisfy you, my dear?”

“Certainly, Henri. Whatever you wish.” She

fluttered her eyelashes, pleased at her ability to seemingly dominate this impenetrable man. "I would like to marry as soon as possible. It pains me to be apart from you."

Odd, Henri thought. *It pains me to be in your presence.* Pushing the thought aside, Henri gallantly offered his arm, and the pair departed the parlor in dignified silence.

Joyously relieved from her task, Adrienne spent the remaining morning, and early afternoon, in the library, indulging in a variety of volumes, each more enlightening than the previous. She made a mental note to ask Henri to borrow some of the tomes, as she was certain Francine would not be frequenting the room.

A shallow knock on the door brought Adrienne from her stupor. "Yes?"

Sabine's slight figure slipped through the narrow crack in the door. "Miss? Mother asks if you would like some lunch. Master Henri and...Mistress Francine took a picnic on their outing."

Setting the book down, Adrienne beckoned her into the room. "Sabine...did you get in any trouble for taking me out last night?"

Clutching her hands together, Sabine hurriedly shook her head. "No, miss."

Adrienne tilted her head to the side. "Sabine, please. Tell me."

"I...oh, miss." Tears flowed freely from her chocolate brown eyes. "Mother knew, and she said I must not bring you again. I said I would not, but I know you can save us from her!"

"My sister?" Adrienne untucked her legs from her skirts, and stood, crossing to the trembling girl. "Sabine, surely you do not believe she is really this...reincarnated mistress of the past?"

"I do! I heard her last night. She will bring down a terrible vengeance on this house!"

Adrienne took Sabine's hands. "The best way to deal with Francine is to appease her. Make sure she has no reason to seek retribution on you, or anyone else. Trust in Master Henri. He will protect you."

Sabine nodded eagerly, wiping tears away with the back of her hand. "Yes, miss. Please come visit often."

Adrienne smiled warmly. "I shall do my best. Now, please tell your mother I would like lunch."

Nodding and curtseying, Sabine scurried from the room, stopping at the door. "If only you were marrying Master Henri. He loves you, I can tell."

"No talk of that, Sabine," Adrienne admonished, but could not prevent her lips from curving.

Sabine smiled back, and ran out.

Trailing her fingers over the chair's brocade, Adrienne circled the room, stopping at Henri's desk. The smooth, polished wood gleamed in the sun streaming through the window, gold locks glinting. It was a handsome piece of furniture, and most likely very costly. She sat in the low-backed chair, placing both hands on the top, imagining Henri sitting here, brow furrowed, going over plantation accounts. She would come into the room, perhaps with a cool drink to tempt him to a momentary break in his work. He might smile lovingly at her, pulling her into his lap for a teasing kiss.

Fisting her hands on the wood, Adrienne slammed them down lightly. The hot prick of tears stung the backs of her eyes. Francine did not deserve such a man. She was vile, and Sabine may have been correct, in a way. Francine would cause destruction, and devastation, to all those in her path, especially if they stood in the way of anything she desired. There would be no peace or happiness for her, or Henri, if they betrayed her.

9

Once the sisters returned to the Beaumont plantation that evening, Francine had set a wedding date for the next month. Arnaud objected there was little time to plan, but his eldest daughter was adamant in her decision.

"June will make a lovely wedding month, Father. Why must you argue with me? You're getting Henri as a son-in-law, a man richer than many of these peasants who surround us!"

"Francine, that is completely unacceptable." Arnaud balled his napkin in his hand.

Tossing her head to the side, Francine scoffed. "It is the truth! Besides, you should see his sugar cane fields, Father. They are so well-tended, despite the slaves' other proclivities."

Adrienne wisely chose to stay silent, again, during her sister's tirade. In the end, her father would acquiesce to her request. Several seamstresses were to be called to the plantation, to work on the lavish gown Francine desired. She wanted something completely new and extravagant, with silk fabric imported from France. Adrienne thought of their mother's gown, carefully packed away in the cedar trunk at the foot of her parents' bed. She resolved, should she ever marry, she would wear that dress, and not burden her father with lofty bills for unnecessary items.

"Adrienne, *petite*, would you like a new dress as well?" Arnaud offered his youngest, wanting to see her treated as well.

"I am sure I have something suitable. The day should be about Francine."

Pleased with her sister's deference, Francine gushed, "It should be gold silk, in the latest French style. After all, Americans would not know style if it bit them!"

The house slaves began clearing the dishes, and Arnaud sighed. "You are American, my dear, by birth. Do not scoff those around you. If you will excuse me, my dears, I have some business to attend to."

Adrienne was unable to ignore her father's hand positioned over his stomach. She excused herself to follow him, before Francine could sweep her into another conversation about dresses. "Father, please, is the pain worse?" She placed a restraining hand on her father's forearm.

"Come this way, my dear." Arnaud ushered his favorite into his study, and shut the door.

Confusion flooded Adrienne's features, as she waited expectantly for an explanation. "Papa?"

"When I arrived home, I sent for the doctor. He fears the ulcers are getting worse, and I may not last the year." Arnaud collapsed back into his chair, with a low groan.

"No, Papa! It cannot be so!" Adrienne rushed to his side, grasping his hand urgently.

Arnaud comforted her the best he could. "Hush, *petite*. That is just one man's opinion. I wish to live long enough to see you married, and happy. I know I objected, but I am glad Francine refuses to delay her marriage."

"Does Monsieur Du Cormier know?"

Arnaud shook his head. "No one, aside from you, knows. I wish it to be kept that way. I have made conditions...new ones for your keeping, laws and propriety be damned. You will have a yearly allowance with what I leave, even though it is not much."

"Oh, Papa, please do not talk this way." Adrienne bit back tears, clutching his hand. "You will just need to rest more."

Arnaud smiled again, caressing Adrienne's face. "So like your mother. You will make a man a loving wife, and perfect mother."

"But, Papa..." Adrienne stopped, refusing to darken her father's mind with the admission of her attraction to Henri. He would feel guilty at his mistake, and it would possibly worsen his condition.

"No, Adrienne. You will be happy. I know in my heart. Now, go to bed, and stop worrying." Arnaud kissed her forehead, and shooed her from the room.

Barely able to control her emotions, Adrienne burst into her bedroom. She collapsed on the bed, and wept for all she had lost, and would soon lose.

"The crop will do well this year, sir. We should be able to harvest soon enough," Isaac Fleming, the overseer of St. Esprit addressed Henri, wiping the sweat from his brow, and replacing his hat. He shifted in the saddle of his chestnut mare.

Henri nodded, looking out across the fields at the slaves working under the hot sun. "Make sure we have extra water. Overheated slaves are no good to me, Fleming."

Fleming was a relic from the old plantation master. He did his job well, using minimal force. All in all, St. Esprit was a good place to live and work. He respected Du Cormier, as the man did not come off as high and mighty, like the last owner. "I hear congratulations are in order, sir."

Adjusting his own hat, Henri peered over at the man. "Yes, I suppose they are. I haven't made any official announcement."

Fleming gestured out to the workers. "They talk, ya see, sir. 'specially since Miss Clotilde is their...well, you know, sir."

"Hmm. Thank you, Fleming. I hope the match will prove worthwhile." Henri squinted, not believing his own words.

"What about Beaumont? I hear things, sir." Fleming hazarded to bring up the topic.

"Too many late nights in the tavern," Henri muttered, soothing his restless horse.

Fleming leaned forward in the saddle. "Ya know, he'll probably marry off the younger one now. She is pretty, sir, if you don't mind me saying."

Henri cleared his throat. "I think we shouldn't be talking about my fiancée's sister in such a frank way, Fleming." His grip tightened on the reins, causing his horse to skitter slightly to the left.

"Sorry, sir."

"I'm going to have a ride around the grounds. I leave things in your capable hands." Henri took off at a trot, trying to work off his restless energy. The thought of Adrienne in the embrace of another man had jealousy rising in his blood. Without thought, he rode towards the tree where he had seen Adrienne before.

Henri smiled as his luck continued. There she sat, beneath the waving branches, head buried in a book. Her golden curls caressed her rosy cheeks, and he felt a tug of longing in his chest. Not wanting to cause her to evade him, as she had done the previous two times they found themselves alone together, he cleared his throat.

Adrienne glanced up, eyes widening at the sight of him. "Oh, Monsieur Du..."

Dismounting, he walked over to her. "Please, do not run away. I can only bear the sight of your fleeing skirts so many times, mademoiselle."

Closing the book over the scrap of fabric she used to mark her place, Adrienne rose to her feet. "Very well. I remain, at both our perils." Her pink lips quirked into a half-smile. "What brings you to Beaumont, sir?"

"I was out for a ride, and wondered if you were enjoying the fresh air as well."

Adrienne threw her head back, tinkling laughter escaping her lips. "You are a terrible liar."

Henri's heart leapt with hope. "It seems your

feelings have softened for me, Adrienne."

Jolting out of her merriment, Adrienne took a step back, clutching the book to her chest. "I...please do not mistake me, sir. I am still resolved in my belief it would be impossible. I have no desire to chase after impossibilities."

"Many say it was impossible for me to own a plantation. I grew up quite poor, Adrienne. I made my way in this world." Henri fingered one of the leaves on the drooping branches. "Never you mind, though. I shall not press the matter. At this moment, I only desire your company. Is that so distasteful?"

"I suppose not." Adrienne lowered herself back to the ground, and Henri did likewise, sitting a few feet away. "Are you prepared for the wedding?" She was determined to keep the conversation polite and disarming.

Henri leaned back, staring out across the small brook nearby. "Is any man prepared to be tied down for the rest of his life? I highly doubt it."

"Oh."

Cursing himself, Henri turned his head. "I did not mean...I mean, I am certain there are some men who would be content to have a wife there waiting for them, but I want more in life. I think you feel the same."

Tapping her fingers against the cover of the book, Adrienne frowned. "I do not feel the same. I would like to be the wife to a man who wants me for me, not someone who dreams of other fanciful pursuits."

"Am I making a mistake, Adrienne? You never responded that day."

Shivering despite the warm weather, Adrienne

desperately wished for a shawl to hide herself from his scrutiny. "I am not to say. It is an arrangement you made with my father for Francine's hand. An impulsive one, at that." She covered her mouth, having spoken much too frankly.

Chuckling, he sat up, facing her. "Impulsive? Explain."

Sucking in a breath, Adrienne forced herself to meet his twinkling eyes. "You chose someone who would make sure your place in our world was secure, without a thought for your own happiness. Francine has the breeding you require, but she will make your life hellish, sir. Of that you can be sure."

Henri sobered, scrutinizing Adrienne carefully. "How is your arm?"

Adrienne clutched the offending limb to her chest, tugging her sleeve. "It will mend, like all things."

Holding out his hand, Henri waited, fixing his eyes on hers. "Let me see."

Glancing around nervously, Adrienne extended her arm, and Henri gently rolled back the loose sleeve. He ran his thumb over the blueish bruises, a frown marring his features.

"I told you it wasn't that bad. I've had worse at her hand." She tugged her arm away, unable to stand the feel of his roving digits.

Henri backed off slightly, dropping his hands into his lap. "I am not a violent man, Adrienne, but your sister will regret it, should she strike me."

Righting her sleeve, Adrienne focused on his impassive face. "I have little doubt she would raise a hand to you, sir. She picks smaller prey...like Sabine..." The name fell from her lips, before she could stop herself.

"Clotilde's daughter?" Henri perked up, immediately concerned. "Would Francine target her anger on a defenseless child?"

"My maids have fallen victim to her wrath many times. My best advice is to tread carefully around her when she's in one of her moods." Adrienne smoothed her skirts.

"I believe I have the answer to my earlier question, Adrienne. If only you were the one I was to marry..." His forthright admission had Adrienne backing away.

Her full lips tremored. "Please...do not...do not say such things." Adrienne's strength was crumbling away. In other circumstances, he might have been close to her side, sharing the murmurs of lovers. She shook her head violently. "No..."

"Adrienne, please forgive me. I have never been a secretive man, a failing on my part, I suppose. I cannot lie, though. At your word, I will break my agreement with Francine, and marry you." He inched up next to her, taking her reluctant hands in his. "You make me happy, Adrienne."

Adrienne felt his calloused hands encompass hers, relishing in their warmth and strength. "Henri...what you suggest would make us outcasts in society..."

"Then I will sell the plantation, and take you elsewhere. We will leave this place."

Adrienne thought of her father, knowing how his condition would worsen under Francine's less than tender care. She would be intolerable, and her father would suffer greatly. Henri's hand rose to her cheek, tracing the smooth skin there. She allowed herself to feel, for a brief moment, leaning her face into his palm, but the reality of circumstances soon had her pulling away.

"No, monsieur. We are not at liberty to cause such distress, especially to my father. You will marry Francine, and I will find a suitable husband. We will be nothing more than friends, from this day forth." Adrienne moved shakily to her feet, unable to control her trembling.

Henri jumped up. "You are cruel, mademoiselle, to bring up such a thought. You in the arms of another man is unthinkable!"

"Well, it is a concept both of us will have to get used to!" Adrienne gasped, as a sob slipped from her lips.

Henri moved forward, taking her shoulders gently. "My sweet girl, are we to live in such misery?"

She extended her hand, and cupped his stubble-roughened cheek. "Yes, Henri, we are, for the sake of our very lives." Rising on tiptoe, she placed a soft kiss on his lips, and withdrew, running across the grass back to the house.

Henri touched his lips, the tingling of her gentle embrace still lingering. One day, he silently vowed, he would have Adrienne as his wife, in this life, or the next.

10

The next few weeks passed in a whirl of silk and flowers. Adrienne found herself wandering aimlessly through the house, her heart emitting an undeniable ache. Arnaud was acutely aware of Adrienne's change, but amounted it to desire to be married as well. He hoped she would be able to gain some interest in one of the eligible young bachelors who would be in attendance at the wedding.

Feigning illness, Adrienne managed to avoid Henri each time he came to the house, and Francine was delighted at his lack of further interest in her sister. Still, his eyes went broody any time her name was mentioned. This vexed her greatly. Determined to put it out of her mind, she concentrated on the design of her new gown.

Standing on a stool, Francine examined her appearance in the mirror, biting her lip. Reclining nearby, Rosalind nibbled on a bonbon, jumping when her friend barked, "Watch your needle, twit!" Her foot flew out, kicking the seamstress in the shoulder.

"Apologies, Mademoiselle Beaumont, for my carelessness."

Rosalind sipped some lemonade, and raised a brow. "Temper, dear Francine. I have been taught a wife should be docile and submissive."

"Ha! Only when she desires something of her husband! I have Henri wrapped around my little finger."

With a vicious smirk, Rosalind delicately wiped her fingers on a handkerchief. "Not what I heard..."

Raising a hand, Francine stayed the seamstress's needle. "Rosalind, I strongly dislike cryptic gossip."

"Well, our overseer said he observed Monsieur Du Cormier in an intimate embrace with your sister." The revelation tickled Rosalind. While she did consider Francine a friend, it gave her great delight to raise the girl's ire.

"Impossible! Why would you believe some grimy overseer? Perhaps he just wanted to slander Henri." Francine turned back to the mirror, admiring her reflection. "Many around here resent his good fortune. He has told me so himself."

"But what if it is true? He marries you, but desires your sister?"

Francine spun, causing the delicate fabric to tear. "Oh, now look what you made me do? I will have Henri know who rules his household. We are going to New Orleans for our honeymoon. I wanted to go to Europe, but he insisted he could not leave the plantation. Still, I shall come back with some lovely purchases. Enough of this suspicion. Should it be true, I will deal with Adrienne appropriately."

Rosalind shrugged. "Then it is none of my business. Will you purchase any slaves in New Orleans? You will need a trustworthy maid."

"I have already told Henri it is a necessity. I would rid the entire house of the current slaves, if I could, but he would not have it. They stare at me in an unsettling way." Francine stilled, so the seamstress could mend the rip with tiny stitches.

Picking another chocolate from the box, Rosalind studied it. "You know, they have strange rites here. You should be careful."

"Oh, Rosalind, enough of the melodramatics. Henri would never keep a slave who posed a threat to his wife."

"And you are quite sure?" Rosalind asked, skeptically.

"Quite! Now, does this dress not enhance my figure in a most alluring way?" The topic of vindictive slaves faded, as Francine imagined how many more fine dresses she would have from Henri's wealth.

Bessie's fine parlor was a welcome retreat for Adrienne, and Sarah's new baby a blessed distraction. As the three ladies conversed, Adrienne cooed over the sweet boy child, whom the couple had named Louis, after George and Elizabeth's father.

"George quite likes Monsieur Du Cormier. He says he has a keen eye for business." Sarah beamed with pride at her husband's complimentary nature.

Adrienne stiffened at the mention of Henri, but continued to rock baby Louis. "Hmm."

Bessie set down her cup of tea. "Addy, dearest, what is wrong? You have been so distant. I know it's not Francine who occupies your time."

Sarah scoffed at the mention of Francine's name, and reached for Louis, who had begun to fuss for his feeding. "I will take the little man here up to feed." Sarah was insistent on feeding the babe herself, much to the shock of the society ladies. Her departure was more to give the friends privacy.

Adrienne waited for the door to shut, before she let the floods of tears forth. Bessie quickly moved to her side, wrapping her in a tender hug. "Oh, my sweet Addy. What troubles you so?"

Breathing in the flowery scent of her dearest friend, Adrienne confided her deepest secret. "Bessie, I am in love."

"In love? Why, how wonderful!" At Adrienne's fallen face, Bessie knew it was not a blessed admission. "Oh, my dearest. With whom?"

The response was barely audible. "Henri Du Cormier."

"Your sister's fiancé? Addy..." Bessie's expression conveyed deep sorrow. "I did not realize you had grown close to him, with so little contact..."

"There were occasions, unknown to my father, and Francine. We met under the willow, once or twice. He confided he wished to marry me instead. I refused him."

Bessie entangled her fingers with Adrienne's. "So you should have! What a cad!"

"Bessie, it is not like that at all. Henri was honest

in his feelings. He wants to be accepted into society, but was willing to give it all up...for me."

"He should never have put you in such a position, if he were a proper gentleman. You must forget, Addy dearest. He will not make your tender affections blossom."

Adrienne gulped loudly. "He has though, Bess. We are so alike. He is educated, despite his lack of social standing and wealth. And he makes me feel...I do not know. It is hard to describe."

"Put him from your mind, Addy. I have wonderful news that will make it easier." Bessie sat back, smiling like a cat with cream. "Sarah's brother is coming to stay from New York. I was hoping to introduce you at the wedding, as George has already gained permission from Henri for him to attend. He is an intelligent man, with many good prospects. Much more attainable than Henri, even if he were attainable."

Adrienne sighed. "I am not sure, Bessie. What is his name?"

"Andrew Dixon. You know Sarah's father does very well in banking. He has Andrew poised to take up a branch in New Orleans. You wouldn't have to leave Louisiana! Besides, Sarah always speaks so highly of him. Give it a chance, Adrienne."

Adrienne clutched her friend's hands. "What about you? Maybe Andrew will fancy you over me. You deserve just as much chance at happiness as I."

"Oh, Addy, I do not care for those things. I am resolved to be a spinster aunt, taking care of all my nieces and nephews."

Adrienne laughed merrily, brushing tears away. "Bessie, you must not be so pessimistic."

"If I find some man kind enough to marry me, I will take him in a heartbeat. For now, I hold little chance, with my brothers scaring off every potential suitor." Bessie waved her hand in the air absently.

"One day, you will find a man they are unable to chase away." Adrienne took a drink of her lukewarm tea, contemplating what Andrew Dixon would be like. After all, Bessie was correct. She did deserve happiness, in some form.

As Adrienne contemplated this notion, the pair heard a loud squeal in the hallway. Sarah burst into the parlor, trailing a man after her. "Oh, Bess! You will never believe it! Andrew surprised me by coming early, and he brought some lovely gifts for little Louis. George, that scoundrel, knew the whole time!"

George sauntered into the room, grinning, bouncing his son in his arms. "What can I say? I do enjoy keeping her on her toes."

Adrienne loved watching the easy interplay between the couple, and thought it would be wonderful to have such an amicable and loving relationship with someone. She raised her eyelashes, and fixed her gaze on the man trailing behind Sarah.

"Oh! Andrew! This is Adrienne Beaumont. Her father owns the plantation you no doubt passed on your way here." She delicately swatted him on the arm, and he mocked pain.

"Easy, sister. It has been a long journey." An easy smile played on his handsome features, an errant lock of chestnut brown hair falling across his lightly-tanned skin. "A pleasure, Miss Beaumont." He bowed his head, cocking it at an angle. "I was unaware the women in Louisiana were so fair. If I had known, I would have arrived even sooner."

Adrienne laughed, certain her cheeks were turning red at his facile tongue and quick wit. "Well, sir, you do certainly present a charming picture," she teased back.

"And they know how to hold their own."

He certainly was not unpleasant to look at. Adrienne watched, as he conversed with Bessie, occasionally glancing back her way.

"Adrienne? My, your head is in the clouds, dear." Bessie patted her hand, drawing her attention back to the conversation.

"Pardon?" Adrienne blinked a few times. "Apologies, Bessie. What were you saying?" Soft laughter filled the room, and she blushed again.

"I wanted to know if you would stay for dinner? I can send a slave back to tell your father."

The reprieve from Francine's latest gown adjustments would be so welcome, and Adrienne agreed immediately. Andrew, standing with George at the fireplace, appeared quite pleased by her answer, as he tickled Louis's chin. Adrienne tried to push away all thoughts of Henri, and center her regard on Andrew.

The remainder of the afternoon passed pleasantly. Despite his trip, Andrew regaled them with stories of New York, where life moved at a speed unknown to those in the small community. There were murmurs of revolt against the abolitionists, and political rioting as the first mayoral election passed. It all sounded exciting to Adrienne, and she felt a draw to visit the illustrious city. Although Andrew seemed to have no political leanings, speaking factually about the events, Adrienne started to see the reason why some people supported abolitionism. She dared not voice her opinions on the matter, but concluded she would find some reading material on the subject, as soon as possible.

Andrew's cordial behavior continued through dinner. He flouted convention, and sat next to her, asking her questions about her life, her parents, and the plantation. His blue eyes, the color of the sky on a clear day, beheld her with rapt attention, not wanting to miss a single word. At the end of the meal, he insisted he would like to walk her home, as the sun still lingered in the sky. Adrienne peered over at Bessie, uncertain about being alone with a man she had just met.

"We will send Jacob along with you. We wouldn't want you to get lost on your way back, Andrew." As always, she elegantly dispelled Adrienne's fears with a simple solution.

The pair departed into the mild evening air. Adrienne remained silent for some time, trying to wrestle with her thoughts, and the reason why she had apparently lost her tongue. Usually one to keep a hold of social situations, she found herself completely lost. It was not so with Henri. Andrew maintained a gentlemanly air, and there was nothing forward, or inappropriate, about his actions on the walk.

"It is very lovely here." His voice broke the lull, and Adrienne startled.

"Oh, yes. I do like to take walks. I can see how it might be boring to someone from New York."

Clasping his hands behind his back, Andrew

directed his gaze upward. "One would think, yes. I assume New Orleans will have some excitement though?"

Adrienne shook her head. "I would not know, sir. I have spent my entire life in the Parish, well, since it was named."

Genuinely shocked, Andrew turned his head to her. "We must remedy that, if you are amiable to a small journey. Sarah is keen to see the city, and George would like to speak to some merchants. I have plans to stay with my sister for several weeks after your sister's wedding."

Taken aback, Adrienne smiled warmly. "I would enjoy that very much."

They reached Beaumont Plantation as the sun was dipping below the horizon. Andrew took her hand, kissing the back. "Thank you very much for allowing me to escort you home. I have to say, it's been a pleasure having such a beautiful companion. May I call on you again?"

She lowered her eyes, her skin warming where he had pressed his lips, nodding her head. "Yes, I should like that. You are attending my sister's wedding, yes?"

"I have more than enough reason to do so, even with an invitation." Waggling his eyebrows, Andrew managed to elicit a giggle from her. Adrienne waited on the porch, waving as he turned off to the path back to Belle Rivière.

Henri stepped from the shadows, with every intention of questioning her, as to the identity of her escort, but decided against it. He circled around the back of the house, trying to ignore how flushed her cheeks were. Yet, there was something missing in her voice. Rubbing his brow, Henri took a roundabout route to the stable, to retrieve his horse. In less than two weeks, he would be married, and could work on not wanting to strangle any man who gazed longingly at Adrienne. Spurring his horse, he galloped off into the night.

Henri cast the cravat across the room in disgust, yelling out to no one in particular his distaste for the piece of clothing. It felt like a noose, tightening slowly around his neck, reminding him of his impending fate.

Benji scooped up the offending object, approaching Henri with caution. “Sir, would you like me to help you?”

Henri sobered, sighing resolutely, and taking it back. “No, no. Thank you, Benji. I think I have a fair bit on my mind.”

Not at liberty to comment on his master’s forthcoming marriage, Benji assisted him into the binding coat. Henri was not himself in these fancy clothes, only worn at the behest of his bride-to-be. He would divest himself of the garments as soon as humanly possible after the wedding. Waving Benji’s hand away, he studied himself for a final moment.

"Send the carriage around, if you would." As Benji left the chamber, Henri dipped his hand into his pocket, pulling out the simple gold band. In a mere hour, he would place it on the finger of a woman he had grown to detest. The past weeks had shown him clearly what she really was like, as he was forced to endure countless parlor talks about the wedding arrangements.

Adrienne avoided him expertly, and he only saw her leaving or returning to the plantation. She chose to spend her time at Belle Rivière, Arnaud informed him. He wondered if it had more to do with the man he had seen her with. Grinding his teeth, Henri shoved the ring back into his pocket.

"The carriage is ready, sir."

Henri lowered his head, following the manservant out. He tightened his hand around the ring. The house slaves had gathered to wish him luck, almost reluctantly. Sabine shifted nervously next to her mother. He smiled encouragingly, nodding to them all as he departed.

Sabine watched Henri disappear through the door, and looked anxiously up at her mother. Clotilde looped her arm around Sabine's narrow shoulders. No words were needed. The company dispersed, all trickling off to do chores around the plantation house in preparation for its new mistress. Sabine watched them all until she was alone.

Reaching beneath her bodice, she withdrew a small pouch. The gris-gris bag contained several strands of Francine's hair, and a ribbon left behind. Charged with a special task by her mother, Sabine climbed the stairs to what would be her new mistress's bedchamber. She fingered the red cloth. Her mother had not allowed her to be present during the making of the bag, worried the *loa* would attach themselves to her innocent daughter.

Cracking open the door, Sabine stepped into the room, shivering despite there being no chill in the air. Sliding her hand between the sheet and the mattress, she placed the bag under the pillow, sending up a silent prayer it would drive the new mistress from the house. Smoothing the covers, Sabine exited the room, running as fast as she could back to her mother.

Clotilde's forearms were sprinkled with flour, as she vigorously kneaded bread dough. Sabine pulled a stool over, and sat upon it.

"Is it done, child?"

Sabine bobbed her head up and down. "Yes, Mama, but will it not harm Master Henri, since he will...couple with her?"

Clotilde ceased her movements. "He may suffer some, but if our prayers are heard, the woman will be gone, and another in her place."

Picking at her nails, Sabine accepted this as she watched Clotilde, wondering what the evening would hold when Mademoiselle Beaumont became their mistress.

"No! The flowers must be on either side of the stairs! Roses! None of these weeds!" Francine hurled another vase at the cowering house slave.

"Miss, please! Your father..."

The following slap was not unexpected. The house slaves were very accustomed to Francine's wrath. Adrienne padded down the stairs, unwilling to accept such abuse on their slaves any longer. She removed the second vase swiftly from Francine's grasp, and peered meaningfully into her vengeful, green eyes.

"Sister, you will cause more distress to yourself. Remember, this is a happy day. Let me find some flowers. I am sure I will not disappoint you." Her melodic voice, reminiscent of their mother, strangely soothed the savage beast.

Francine blinked, unwillingly feeling her anger fading. "Yes...please. Perhaps I am merely overwhelmed by the events."

"The wedding is not for a few hours yet. Please, allow Hetty to draw you a cool bath. It will take the heat from the day." She waved over her own maid, who had trailed after the young mistress in her quick flight.

Hetty, in all her grace and glory, escorted the unusually placid Francine up the stairs, as Adrienne turned to face the poor woman hiding by the bannister. She waved her out, placing a hand on the woman's cheek.

"Magnolias, Chloe. The scent is fresh, and they are plentiful in the garden."

Chloe beamed at Adrienne, thinking this would be the last day she would be subject to the abuse at the hands of Francine. "Yes, miss. Thank you, miss." She gathered the broken shards and hurried away, lest the demon return.

"What is this hullabaloo, *ma petite*?" Arnaud emerged from his study, his cravat askew.

Adrienne smiled lovingly at her father, her swift fingers straightening the awkwardly squint tie. “Nothing, Papa. I have made all right.”

Arnaud’s eyes misted. “You sound so like your mother, Adrienne, but I have told you that on many occasions. How is Francine?”

“Pacified, for the time being. I do believe there is a heart beneath all those brambles.” She smoothed the cravat. “There.”

“Ah, yes, it did need a woman’s touch.” He stepped back to admire his youngest daughter. “I know how much you insisted on not having a new gown, but this one suits you well.”

Adrienne twirled like a child showing off a new party dress. The floral patterned, pink fabric fell in elegant lines around her slender form. The sleeves formed soft ruffles above her elbows, leaving her forearms bare. Around her neck, she wore a simple pearl necklace, which had once belonging to her mother. Hetty had worked tirelessly to sweep the blonde locks into an elaborate braided style, adorned with delicate, pink blossoms.

“Very much a young woman, *ma petite*. No longer a child. Shall I be watching our door for suitors?”

Adrienne blushed, her first thought of Henri, despite the impossibility of the notion. “It is possible, Papa.”

Arnaud wound Adrienne’s arm through his, as they took a turn about the entryway. “You have been spending a great deal of time at Bessie’s. Is it possible something there draws you?” His eyes held a mischievous glint.

“Oh, Papa! Bessie is delightful company.”

"And Madame Forrest's brother?" Lines emerged around his eyes, as he suppressed a budding grin.

"Papa! Andrew...Monsieur Dixon is a perfect gentleman, who happens to enjoy walking in the gardens as much as I do." Adrienne's cheeks glowed the same color as her dress.

Andrew had always been pleasant and proper, keeping their interactions within the bounds of societal norms. However, he tended to speak of banking frequently, and his adventures in New York, barely taking time to discover her inner desires. He would make a perfect, doting husband, as long as she remained docile and obedient.

Arnaud wiggled his eyebrows, standing in front of her. "As long as whomever you choose makes you happy, I will always approve." He kissed his daughter's hand, and returned to his study, the only sanctuary he had from the bustling wedding preparations.

"Is that what you truly want? A perfect gentleman?" Henri strode over, raking his gaze over her. "You look very nice."

Raising her hand, Adrienne started fiddling with her necklace. "I did not hear you come in."

He chuckled. "You never seem to hear me approach. Dixon...is this the illustrious brother-in-law of George Forrest? Has that been why you have been fleeing to Belle Rivière every day?"

Pressing her lips together, Adrienne moved to Chloe, who was arriving with a vase of magnolias. "Thank you, Chloe." She placed them on an end table, leaning down to draw in the scent. She straightened, gasping as Henri was right at her back.

"Is he more appealing than I?" he murmured, leaning close.

Adrienne's heart beat rapidly at his proximity to her person. He smelled of soap and masculinity. "He is not promised to another."

Henri growled, and walked towards Arnaud's study. "I will go announce myself to your father. Will you please inform your sister I am here? We will be leaving for the church soon, no doubt."

The door shut quietly, but the sound deafened Adrienne. She slouched forward, a hand over her stomach, gasping for breath. Drawing on an unknown inner strength, Adrienne righted herself and ascended the stairs, rapping softly on Francine's door.

"Who is it?" Her sharp tone came from inside the chamber.

Adrienne touched the handle, considering opening the door, but decided to call through instead. "Francine, Monsieur Du Cormier is here. He asked me to tell you."

"He is not supposed to see me before the ceremony!" Francine ripped the door open, half-dressed in a tightly cinched corset and pantalets.

Adrienne stepped back. "He had business to attend to with Papa. I am sure they will depart before us."

Francine swept her gaze downward. "That dress...where did you get it?"

"Papa had it made for me."

The door slammed in her face, and Adrienne heard screaming coming from within the room. "Rosalind! You should see her! I look like a frump compared to her. It is meant to be my day."

Rosalind had arrived shortly after breakfast to assist the bride in her preparations, meaning she sat on the suite, and ate candied oranges. "Tosh! She is a child, hardly going to draw the eye of any respectable gentleman."

"You are an apt liar, Ros."

The conversation turned to Francine's dress, and Adrienne solemnly trekked down the hallway to her room. She leaned against the closed door, scanning the room until her eyes landed on her mother's portrait.

"Mama...you smelled of magnolias..." The tears fell unheeded.

July, 1834

Adrienne rode with Rosalind and Francine in subdued silence. Admittedly, Francine suited her extravagant gown, and the wedding bonnet trimmed in lace added the proper accessory to the many layered confection. She traced the embroidery with her eyes, carefully avoiding being caught.

"Adrienne, tell us about Monsieur Forrest's brother-in-law. Is he engaged?" Rosalind's otherwise beautiful complexion twisted into a most ugly expression.

Coughing into her gloved hand, Adrienne skimmed the passing scenery. "He is amicable, certainly, with no ties, romantic or otherwise. His father wishes him to invest in a bank in New Orleans."

"Oh, hmm, isn't that fascinating, Francine?"

Francine scowled under her bonnet. "Quite." Rosalind wisely bit back her comments for the remainder of the journey.

They arrived at the church, the remaining guests being ushered inside. Several paused to steal a glimpse at the famed wedding gown. Rosalind's presently silent tongue had been wagging for the previous weeks. The coachman assisted the three ladies from the conveyance, and departed.

"Luck, my pet." Rosalind cooed, kissing Francine on the cheek, and scurrying into the church, fan flapping.

In a rare moment of confidence between sisters, Francine grimaced at the retreating form. "How I despise her at times."

"She certainly does take some tolerance." Adrienne passed her now pale sister a bouquet of flowers. "I do wish you happiness. Let him make you happy." She regretted the words instantly.

"I will know nothing of happiness under that roof." Lifting her skirts, Francine ascended the steps to the church, as the organ music blared out.

Adrienne followed obediently, stopping in the doorway. Arnaud offered his eldest daughter his arm, to escort her to her soon-to-be husband. As the pair walked towards the altar, Adrienne met Henri's eyes, glassy and emotionless. She quickly fell into step behind her father and sister, sliding into a seat next to Bessie. Her steadfast friend clasped her hand reassuringly, and Andrew beamed at her from beside Sarah.

The preacher's blessings droned in her head, as she tried with all her being to avoid staring at

Henri's stiffened shoulders. He had not missed Andrew's adoring gaze, and she knew Henri's eyes burned through her gown. Should she have been laid bare, naked as a newborn babe, on the altar, she would have felt less vulnerable than she did in that moment.

The crowd surged to its feet, Adrienne dragged unwillingly with Bessie, as cheers of congratulations and good fortune filled the church. They would return to the Beaumont Plantation for celebrations, and then Henri would whisk his new bride to St. Esprit. That would be the end of it all, and life could move steadily along.

Andrew offered to escort her from the church, and she gratefully leaned on his strong arm for support, not caring if he misconstrued the gesture. Henri and Francine vanished into the back of a carriage, and the guests sought out their own means of transportation to the festivities. Andrew gallantly relinquished her into the care of her father with a bow.

Once inside their own carriage, Arnaud broached the subject. "Andrew Dixon is certainly a gentleman, *ma petite*."

"Yes, Papa. He has always been cordial to me whenever I visit Bessie."

"My daughter, you have not been yourself of late. I heard you weeping last night in your room. Please, be honest with me. Has Andrew harmed you in some way you are concealing from me?" Arnaud reached for his daughter's hand.

Adrienne vigorously shook her head, eyes flicking upward to stop the treacherous tears. "No, Papa, never. As I said, he has been nothing but kind and attentive."

"Then what? Please, have I done something to upset you?"

"Oh, no, Papa. It's just...I...I wish I could be married, like Francine. I feel ready to have my own family, and bless you with grandchildren to sit on your knee." The lie flew from her lips, much safer than admitting the horrible truth.

Arnaud smiled, relieved. "Perhaps you will not have long to wait, and Monsieur Dixon will make an honorable offer of marriage. He is certainly keen on you, and would make an excellent husband."

"Yes, Papa." Adrienne smiled through her pain, not understanding the emotions she harbored towards Henri. He made her feel something Andrew never could.

Henri leaned back in the carriage seat, scrutinizing his new wife. If he was not mistaken, fear hid behind her green eyes, but it was soon replaced with malice.

"You wished it were her, did you not?" The words spat hatefully from her mouth.

Lighting a cigar, Henri lazily blew the smoke towards the open window. "I do not know what you mean, madame."

Ripping the bonnet from her head, Francine would have crushed it beneath her slippered foot, had there been more space in the carriage. "My sister! I am second best! You settled for me because of what I can give you. I despise you!"

"This is hardly the time to work yourself up, my dear. Wait until I have bedded you before you decide what an abhorrent mate I will be." His lips quirked into a smile, knowing his comments enraged her further.

Francine's cheeks took on a rosy hue, despite her efforts to conceal her irritating desire for the man. "How dare you speak so to me?"

"I dare because I am your husband. Now, compose yourself. We will arrive to a room full of guests shortly. They will want to see a demure, blushing bride. Not the raging leviathan I have before me."

His wife duly silenced, Henri contemplated the end of his cigar. The image of Adrienne framed in the church door, bathed in sunlight haunted his memory. How he wanted to gouge out Andrew Dixon's eyes as he devoured her, and tear off his hands for ever having touched his ethereal beauty.

The carriage drew to a shaky halt outside the house. Henri dutifully assisted his wife from the interior, pulling her reluctant arm through his. Plastering on mutual expressions of joy, Henri and Francine entered the ballroom.

Applause resounded throughout the decorated room, and Arnaud stepped forward, glass raised. "To Monsieur and Madame Du Cormier. May they have many wonderful years together!"

Echoes of his toast sounded, and more glasses were lifted, as a house slave served the couple. Henri gladly accepted the champagne in hopes the alcohol would temper his emotions. However, as guests surrounded Francine, wishing her well, he had a moment to skim the room, his eyes landing on Adrienne, next to Andrew Dixon. Francine impatiently drew his attention back to the crowd of guests, introducing him to several influential landowners.

George Forrest clapped Henri on the shoulder. "Congratulations, Henri. I wish you both the very best. And who knows? I may be welcoming your sister-in-law into my own family shortly."

Henri's hand curled into a fist, as he did his best to relax his tense facial muscles. "Yes, Adrienne seems quite taken with your brother-in-law."

"As is he with her. He wants to ask to court her properly this evening. Wonderful news, eh?" George was blissfully unaware of the jealous animosity radiating from his new friend.

"Indeed." Henri reached for another glass of the fizzy alcohol, nearly downing it, as George returned to his little family, Sarah clinging to his arm adoringly.

Unexpected panic rose in Henri's chest, as Andrew started to lead Adrienne over, apparently to wish his congratulations on the couple. He damned himself for ever agreeing to let the man attend his wedding, but he had been unaware of his affections towards Adrienne. Briskly, Henri excused himself to seek some air.

Curling his fingers around the railing of the balcony, Henri sucked in the humid summer air, glaring out across the treetops. He envied the freedom of the flocks of birds circling the brook along the Beaumont property. A soft voice broke him from his brooding.

"It is usually the other way around, when we find ourselves in this situation."

He turned, leaning back, and watched Adrienne glide towards him. "Yes, it is."

"Henri...Monsieur Du Cormier..." Her mouth opened and closed, struggling to find the right words.

"Henri. We are family now, Adrienne." Her blonde curls caught the sunlight, and he blinked, trying to calm his restless soul.

Adrienne clasped her hands together. "Yes, I suppose you are correct. Henri, I do not wish this to be the end of our friendship. I know..." Her voice failed her.

"Adrienne...I will not, nay, cannot stop my feelings for you, but I know you need to seek your own contentment in this life, so I will not press on you further. What is done, is done." Henri knew his sentiment flowed with falsehoods, aside from loving her.

Her face relaxed in increments. "It is good to hear you say those words." Bowing her head, Adrienne departed. Little did Henri know, she was battling the same crushing emotions as he.

Andrew crossed the ballroom to meet Adrienne as she re-entered, taking her hand in his. "Ah, there you are. I needed to speak with you. Your father has given us leave of the parlor. I can find a chaperone, should you wish?"

Unable to trust herself for the moment, Adrienne nodded. "I believe Bessie is around."

"Excellent. I shall fetch her, and meet you there." He kissed her hand warmly, and raced off.

Adrienne wandered through the crowds, hardly seeing anything before her swimming eyes, and somehow reached the tranquility of the parlor. She sat on one of the burgundy brocade chairs, waiting for Andrew and Bessie. Peeling the gloves from her shaking hands, Adrienne laid them aside on one of the polished wood tables. Her mother had so often received visitors, seated on this very chair. She tucked back a wayward strand of hair as the door opened, following a brief knock.

"Addy?" Bessie moved into the room, with Andrew at her heels.

Straightening, Adrienne gestured to the seats opposite her. "Thank you, Bess." Her eyes held another, unspoken meaning, and Bessie nodded kindly.

Andrew chose to stand, pacing restlessly. The women watched him, knowing he was grappling with the proper words. Finally, he stopped, kneeling by Adrienne's side. "Adrienne...Miss Beaumont...Adrienne..."

Laughing softly, but not in a condescending way, Adrienne touched his sleeve. "Adrienne is fine."

"Oh, yes, I was not sure...anyway, I would ask for the honor of courting you, exclusively, with intentions to marry you, should you be agreeable to the arrangement."

Bessie beamed, nodding eagerly behind Andrew's back. The match would be suitable. Andrew had high prospects, but Adrienne was not sure she merely wanted a marriage because it was worthy and fitting.

"Have you spoken to my father? I feel he should be..."

Andrew smiled. "That is something I admire so much about you, Adrienne. You desire to adhere to tradition and propriety. I have spoken to your father, yes, and he is highly agreeable to the arrangement, should you consent. Do you?" His sky blue eyes searched hers eagerly, hoping for the answer he so desperately sought.

"I...may I please have a moment to speak to Bessie? I would want my dearest friend's advice."

Baffled, Andrew stood, but bowed his head. "I shall give you some time." He smiled nervously at Bessie, departing the room.

As soon as the door clicked shut, Bessie rushed to Adrienne's side. "Are you mad?" she hissed anxiously. "Is this about...Du Cormier? You must not hold hope there. We both know Francine would destroy anyone involved in a liaison between you and Du Cormier!"

Adrienne crumpled forward, head cradled in her palms. "Oh, Bess, I know you are right. I know Andrew would be, by all standards, an excellent catch. Could I learn to be happy with him?"

"Yes, my sweet friend!" Bessie gently lowered Adrienne's hands. "You will learn, and eventually come to love Andrew."

Drawing in a steadying breath, Adrienne nodded. "Please fetch Andrew, and then leave us."

Bessie smirked slightly, believing to know why the couple would wish privacy. She hurried out the door, and seconds later, Andrew replaced her presence in the room. He crossed to Adrienne, resuming his position.

Adrienne forced herself to relax. "Andrew, our strolls together and conversation has been quite pleasing. You must know, I do not love you now, but mayhap, with time, I could grow to do so. To answer your question, yes, I consent to your offering." Her voice sounded foreign, her tongue struggling over the words.

Andrew, however, noticed no distress in his companion, moving swiftly to his feet and taking her hands. He pulled her standing, placing his lips to the soft skin. "I will endeavor to do all I can to earn your love, Adrienne. May I kiss you?"

Nodding her permission, Andrew dipped his head, placing his lips on hers. He lifted his head again, peering down at her for approval. Adrienne plastered an accommodating smile, and he escorted her back to the ballroom.

13

St. Esprit loomed in the distance, illuminated by the full moon. The carriage rocked gently, as the horses' hooves crackled on the dirt drive. The interior atmosphere of the conveyance was tense. Francine did her best to avoid making eye contact with her new husband, mixed emotions swirling in her head. The gathered guests at her wedding were solicitous, but when Andrew Dixon gloriously made public his intentions to court Adrienne, the attention shifted. What was meant to be her day was ruined by her perfect sister.

Henri ignored her, puffing away on a vile cigar, not caring she remained silent. Her fingernails left half-moon circles in her palms as she clenched her fists in rage, but there was no time to voice her indignation. The carriage came to a jerky halt, and the door opened. Henri descended, tossing away the cigar. He held out his hand obligingly, and she exited as well, glancing around at the blazing lanterns on the porch, along with the gathered house slaves. She fixed her gaze on the young slave girl, Sabine.

"Henri, dearest. I would very much like that young girl for my maid." She extended a finger, pointing at the shuddering child.

Henri nodded curtly, turning to speak with a tall man Francine recognized as his personal valet, Benji. "Yes, as you wish. Sabine will serve Mistress Du Cormier from now on."

Francine ascended the steps, ignoring the other slaves. "Come along, Sabine. I will instruct you in my needs."

Clotilde had to give Sabine a subtle shove on the back to get the girl's feet moving, and she shuffled after Francine. Once inside her private chambers, away from prying eyes, Francine grasped the girl's arm, nails digging into the coffee colored skin of the trembling slave. "You will do as I say, at all times, without question. If you refuse, I will have you beaten and sold off to some barley farmer, who will work you to exhaustion during the day, and abuse you mercilessly at night. Are we clear?"

Sabine fought the tears, although her dark eyes dampened. "Yes, mistress." She never imagined one person could have so much evil permeating her being.

"Now, I require a hot bath. My trunks have been brought over, as you see. Each garment to be treated with care. They are certainly worth more than you."

Francine sat primly at the vanity, removing her bonnet. "Oh, and be quick about it! I do not want to keep my husband waiting."

Sabine only just remembered to bob a curtsey before her mistress's disapproving glare, before scampering from the room, down to the kitchens. Clotilde was waiting, and wrapped her arms comfortingly around the child, as heaving sobs wracked her daughter's body.

"Hush, hush now. You must never let her see your weakness. We are strong, *ma belle fille*. Now, she is wanting a bath, yes? I have already made preparations. Your survival will depend on the ability to anticipate her ever changing moods. Little did she know, she has picked an excellent maid." Caressing her daughter's face, Clotilde raised Sabine's chin. "Your mama will never see you sold."

"How...?" Sabine faltered, catching up a corner of her apron to wipe away the tears.

"Your mama knows all. Now, take these linens. They have been warmed." Pressing the cloths into Sabine's hand, she shooed her back up the stairs.

Francine was removing her jewelry carefully, placing it in a velvet lined box. Moving to the adjoining room, Sabine noted the bath tub was already full, lightly scented with lavender. She briskly dipped a hand in, please it was at the proper temperature, and returned to her mistress.

"If you would, madame, your bath is ready. May I assist you in removing your clothing?"

Visibly pleased with the polite tone, Francine allowed Sabine to divest her of her clothing, and settle her into the bath. Lowering her eyes, Sabine begged to be excused to prepare her night garments and pack away the delicate gown. When consent was given, she left the bathing chamber, and busied herself with the tasks at hand.

Folding the dress so as to not harm the delicate lace and fabric, Sabine peered over every so often to see if Francine required her. There was no doubt her mistress was a beautiful woman, but her ugly behavior subtly took away from her being a true beauty, like her sister. Sabine missed the kind woman, and secretly hoped she would visit soon.

Francine barely shifted when Sabine was at her side, a warmed drying cloth in her hands. "Hmm, thank you, Sabine." The sentiment was issued more as a courtesy than a genuine expression of gratitude.

Sabine carefully patted her mistress dry, holding a sheer laced nightgown ready for her to put on. "May I brush your hair out, madame? I will make it shimmer for you."

Her threats really must have frightened the young girl, as Francine noted the requests were meant to please her alone. "Yes, it is sore pinned so tightly to my scalp."

Sabine meticulously removed the curved pins holding the curls in place. They tumbled elegantly down Francine's back. Picking up the silver backed hair brush, Sabine worked her way carefully through them, taking every precaution not to tug on any snarls. By the time she finished, ebony locks did indeed shine in the low candlelight.

A low rap on the door had Francine fluffing her hair and smoothing her night gown. "Get out," she hissed. Sabine curtseyed and opened the door, curtseying again as Henri entered the room. He nodded to the girl, and Sabine scurried off, carrying the sodden linens from the bath. Carefully raking his gaze over his wife, Henri admitted she was a beauty, voluptuous in the right places. Maybe the marriage would not be a total disappointment after all.

Crossing the room, Henri drew Francine towards him, disappointed when her body stiffened. He wondered if it was virginal fear, so he tried to allay her fears with a kiss. Her lips did not soften under his. "Francine, are you well? Perhaps we should stop until we are more comfortable with each other?"

She curled her hands at her sides. "No, we must. People will talk if they realize."

Henri furrowed his brow. "As you wish, madame, but you must relax. You are like a stone slab." He encircled her waist with his arm, drawing her into his embrace.

Francine's stomach threatened to heave. She did not enjoy these attentions at all. "Can I not lay on the bed? And you may do what you need to do?"

Without meaning to, Henri chuckled. "It is usually more pleasurable if you are prepared. Otherwise, it can be quite painful."

Balking, Francine scowled. "Painful?"

"When I enter your body."

Francine broke away, moving swiftly to the bed. "I would rather it be done and over with. Then we might never do it again unless to conceive a child."

All attraction for his bride vanished. Henri did not wish for an icicle in his bed. However, if this is what she wished, he would oblige. Stripping off his shirt, he motioned to the neatly made bed. "After you, madame."

Adrienne set her novel aside, staring out the large window in the library as a lavish carriage approached along the drive. It had been several weeks since Francine's marriage, and she had not been back to the plantation house once. The relief was palatable, and the household went about in a more relaxed manner. Even Helene's meals seemed to taste better. Andrew made daily visits, planning with joy the impending trip to New Orleans. Bessie, George, and Sarah would be joining them, and Adrienne's father was more than pleased with the named chaperones.

A house slave knocked on the library door, opening it after Adrienne issued permission. "Pardon, miss, but your sister has arrived. She is asking for you."

Adrienne set aside her book, smoothing her blue day dress. "Thank you. Please have refreshments brought." Hustling from the room, she made her way to the small parlor.

Francine paced restlessly, her green traveling dress rustling with every step. "I see the slaves have grown lazy in my absence, sister."

Serene as ever, Adrienne bobbed her head. "It is good to see you as well, Francine. Does marriage agree with you?"

"Certainly not! It is a horrible invention of man!" She slumped into a chair. "I am bored out of my mind! Henri is away all the time, and Rosalind, well, she rarely ventures to see me. I am resolved to come visit my sister."

Adrienne frowned, pressing her lips together. "You are always welcome here, Francine. Surely it cannot be all horrors, as you say?"

A slave quickly entered the room, placing the tea service and tray of cakes, departing just as swiftly. Adrienne crossed over, pouring cups for herself and Francine.

"Oh, but it is! And the marriage bed...be thankful you are not wed, sister!"

An involuntary shiver crept down Adrienne's spine. She had had a few illicit thoughts of bedding Henri, late at night when sleep eluded her. "Is he not a kind husband?"

"I often wish for the act to be over! I know I must give him children, but the mere thought turns my stomach!" Francine sipped her tea.

Adrienne set her cup down, changing the subject. "Are you looking forward to the trip to New Orleans? Andrew mentioned you would be joining us."

"Ah, yes, our belated honeymoon," Francine grumbled, in a most unladylike fashion. "I do hope to get some new dresses while we are there."

Rolling her eyes as Francine inspected the trim on her gown, Adrienne retrieved her tea, nearly dropping it at her sister's question.

"Are you going to marry him? I hear he is going to be very prosperous in the banking business."

"Every person I speak to seems to think so. As for marriage, I am not sure. He has asked." The revelation of the proposal had been kept from all, including Bessie. Even Adrienne herself was unsure as to why she divulged the information now, and to a most unlikely recipient. "I suppose it will be a topic of discussion on the trip," she added quickly.

Francine made an indifferent noise, and Adrienne could not determine if it was approval or disdain. "Well, I presume it will remain to be seen. If I were you, I would marry in New Orleans. There is no point having a lavish ceremony, as I have already stolen any possible way you could top my wedding."

Adrienne opened her mouth to retort, when their father entered the room. "Pardon me, ladies, but I heard my eldest daughter had come to visit." Arnaud held out his hands, drawing Francine to her feet, and placing a kiss on her cheek. "It is lovely to see you."

"I am sure, Father. Did you hear Mr. Dixon has asked for Adrienne's hand? Isn't that a bit unorthodox since he hasn't spoken to you?" Her prim tone had Adrienne wanting to throw her hot tea at her sister's smug face.

Arnaud tilted his head, meeting Adrienne's clear blue eyes with hidden wonder, and a subtle wink. "Why, yes, I was aware. I think it would be a marvelous match."

Unexpectedly defeated, Francine reached for her hat. "I must be off. I have lots to pack for this trip. I do hope Mr. Dixon has planned enough transportation." She left with little fanfare, leaving Arnaud smiling reassuringly at his daughter.

"I had an inkling, *ma petite*, but I wanted to wait for you to tell me." Arnaud took Francine's vacated seat.

Adrienne directed her gaze downward, wringing her hands. "I like Andrew, Papa, but I fear he is overzealous in his pursuit. I understand from Bessie he receives near daily letters from his father, asking about his 'situation.'"

Arnaud frowned. "He has not been forthright with me either in his full intentions. I merely ask you be cautious now. I have heard stories; things I did not wish to bring up in front of your sister."

"Papa, what can you mean? You have always been honest with me!" Adrienne sat forward in the chair. "And you would let me go away with him?"

"You will be well-escorted. Think nothing of what I said. I am a foolish old man who listens to rumors." Arnaud waved his hand. "Now, you must pack. Take Hetty with you." He stood, slightly hunched, and left the room, leaving Adrienne wondering about the mysterious stories.

"Damn!" she swore, slamming the delicate china down, in awe it did not shatter in her hand.

"You have been very quiet, Addy. What troubles you?" Bessie rocked gently to the motion of the carriage.

Shifting her gaze away from the rolling scenery and plantation homes, Adrienne smiled. "Nothing out of the ordinary. I am merely anticipating our time in the city. I have never stayed in a hotel before."

Andrew leaned back against his seat opposite her. "You will love it, Adrienne darling. It is sublime."

Sarah nodded in agreement. "I remember Father taking us to tea at one in New York. So lavish! I could barely contain myself!"

"You were seven, sis." Andrew shook his head with a grin, twisting the ring on his pinkie finger. "Everything was lavish in your eyes, and you never contained yourself." He teased her so easily, causing the color to rise on her cheeks.

"Anyway, why are you not riding with the other men? I cannot believe Francine chose to have a carriage on her own. Is she always so disagreeable, Adrienne?" Sarah questioned, throwing her discarded apple core at her brother.

Adrienne's lips curved. "It is never polite to speak ill of your family."

"That's a 'yes,' for those of you unaware of Francine's lovely disposition." Bessie laughed. "Yes, Sarah, she is frightfully disagreeable, and I doubt we shall see much of her on this journey."

Andrew held the apple core up in disgust. "Must you act so unladylike? I see why Father shipped you out to slave country."

Sarah gasped, and the topics of Francine, and Adrienne's silence, were forgotten, descending into stories about the siblings' childhood in New York.

The party stopped for a picnic lunch, to help break up the nearly thirty-mile journey. Spreading blankets beneath a tree, Adrienne paused to watch Henri and Andrew walking nearby, heads low in serious discussion. Andrew jerked back, throwing up his arms, and returning to her side. He caught an edge of the blanket, and helped her settle it on the ground.

"Did you have a disagreement?" Adrienne glanced back to see Henri, arms crossed, glowering in their direction.

Andrew retrieved a basket of food from Hetty. "It's not to trouble yourself with, Adrienne. Men's business."

Her brow creased. She hated it when men

assumed women were pretty play things to adorn drawing rooms. “Sit and have something to eat. Where have George and Sarah run off to?”

Waggling his brows, Andrew leered at her. “To have some time alone, I suspect.”

Adrienne opened her mouth to retort when Henri, Francine, and Bessie joined them.

“Are we to eat like savages?” Francine groaned, arranging her skirts to sit.

Henri leaned against the tree. “It is a beautiful day.” He locked eyes with Adrienne. “We should enjoy it before we get to the city.”

The tension in the air was thick as the company ate in silence, listening to the wind rustle the branches, and the birds singing in the sunshine. Before long, George and Sarah returned, all blushes and smiles. George shrugged, explaining the new baby had not left them much time to be alone. The clarification of their absence had everyone, even Francine, in stitches of laughter. Sated from their fare, the youthful party boarded the carriages once more, and continued on to New Orleans.

Henri watched the employees of the hotel direct the unloading of their bags and assignments of rooms. Francine begged indulgence as she was suffering from a headache due to the journey. He had grown used to her headaches, having experienced their effects nightly since their wedding. His hand slowly clenched into a fist as Andrew wrapped his arm around Adrienne’s narrow waist. He had urged the young man to show caution in his business investments, reminding him there were many gamblers and thieves in New Orleans. His concerns had been rudely rebuffed.

George clapped him on the back. "Well, old boy, it seems we have some time while the ladies freshen up. Care to get a drink?"

Henri coughed, straightening his coat. "Sounds like a good idea. Is there a bar in the hotel?"

Nodding, George walked into the establishment, admiring the décor. "Certainly is something. I haven't been to New Orleans since before I married Sarah. The city has changed."

Subtly inclining his head, Henri's face darkened as Andrew joined them, a grin on his face. "Congratulate me, boys! I'm to be married."

Suppressing the urge to put his fist through the gold leaf wallpaper, Henri forced a smile as George issued the appropriate felicitations, insisting on treating the men to a glass of quality, imported whiskey, certainly not cheap.

"Adrienne certainly is a catch. When will you wed?"

Andrew rolled the liquor around his tongue. "Tomorrow. I wanted to go tonight, but she insisted on needing time to rest."

Henri's grip tightened on his glass, downing the drink in one. The men looked at him agog, and he shrugged. "Women."

"I should insist. Then I can bed her tonight." The potent liquor had gone straight to the younger man's head.

"Another!" Henri's hoarse voice interrupted any thoughts of the virile young man bedding his sweet Adrienne. His Adrienne? He must really stop thinking of her as his possession. She belonged to another, or would, soon enough.

A youthful boy, with skin the color of caramel, approached their table, handing a note to George. He nodded dismissively, opening the paper. "It seems our ladies are begging pardon, and wish to have a quiet meal in their rooms tonight."

Andrew hit his fist on the table with glee. "Excellent! We must explore the town, and see what the nightlife has to offer! If I cannot bed my fiancée this night, I will find a suitable whore."

George did not appear to be shocked by these words, but Henri felt anger rising in his blood. The true nature of Andrew Dixon was bursting forth rapidly. The stories he had related to Arnaud had not reached Adrienne's ears. Perhaps there was not time. Still, he resolved to keep a close eye on his companion.

Henri stood. "I had better bid Francine farewell. It would be another thing for her to hold against me in unknown slight."

The other men laughed, but Henri remained impassive. He climbed the carpeted staircase to the suite he shared with his frigid wife. As expected, she was laying in the bed, cloth over her eyes, while her maid fanned her delicately.

"I am leaving with George and Andrew. I should return later this evening."

She waved her hand indifferently, and Henri closed the door. Shock penetrated him to the core when Adrienne emerged from her room. "Mademoiselle. I hear congratulations are in order." He bowed aristocratically.

Adrienne stopped abruptly. "Oh, yes, thank you.

Are you departing for the evening?" A curl had escaped a hairpin, and dangled provocatively along her exposed collarbone.

"Yes. George and Andrew wish to celebrate."

Her finger wound around the stray lock of hair, drawing his attention acutely to her creamy skin. "Will you be going far? I worry Andrew has little restraint."

Ah! Perhaps her father had warned her after all. "Not far. Next door is a respectable establishment." The lie permeated his lips, not wanting to trouble Adrienne with the sordid details of gentleman's clubs.

"Then I bid you a pleasant evening." She curtseyed, quickly departing his company for the lavatory.

Henri cursed the growing lust in his body, damning it back. Upon rejoining the men, he found Andrew already intoxicated, and loudly voicing his desire to go to the brothel. George glanced around, embarrassed, dragging his brother-in-law from the hotel. Henri reluctantly followed, double checking to make sure the pepperbox pistol was tucked under his coat. One could not be too careful in a city like New Orleans.

The noises of the city kept Adrienne awake long into the night. Resigning herself to the fact she would not get any rest that evening, she crept from her room, crossing the hall to where Andrew should be sleeping. Her knocks on the door went unanswered, and her brow wrinkled in confusion. He should have returned, as they were to be wed in the morning. Surely he should be in fit condition for the lifelong vows they would exchange.

She crossed back to her room, hastily putting on a dress, slippers, and a black cloak. Weaving through the other patrons at the hotel bar, she realized what a lively place New Orleans became at night, and something tugged at her to go back and find a suitable escort. She inquired politely at the reception desk for the whereabouts of her companions, and was pointed to the establishment next door.

"You really should not go out alone, mademoiselle. Please, allow me to send one of our boys with you." The suited man insisted, and Adrienne found herself in the humid summer evening air accompanied by a boy, who was no doubt a slave, though smartly dressed.

"If you please, miss. Wait here, and I will go inside. It's no place for a lady, miss."

Adrienne shifted nervously under the glare of so many men out for the evening. There were some women, but they were surely ladies of the night, flitting in and out of dark crevices. Her attention was drawn to some yelling, and she went to investigate, fighting her own good senses. As she turned a corner, she spotted a familiar man bending over another, who lay prone on the dirt.

Adrienne's scream pierced the black night. Jumping up, Henri hurriedly grabbed her by the arm, hauling her away from the prying gaze of the gathered people. "Hush! How did you get here? Are you mad?"

Her vision came into focus, and she immediately

recognized the man, clearly dead. She frantically gestured to the body of Andrew, blood seeping through his white shirt. Her voice caught in her throat, as she visibly paled, swooning into Henri's arms. He gently tapped her cheeks, her fluttering eyelids finally opening. "He's dead," she managed to force between her bloodless lips.

Henri righted her, taking her fevered face in his cool hands. "Yes, Adrienne, he is."

Adrienne spotted the pistol tucked in his flapping coat. Trembling violently, she clawed at his grasp. "You...you..."

"No! Not I! A knife, I swear!" His body tensed, as if restraining himself. "Stop it, Adrienne. You will draw blood." He removed his hands, steadying her with an arm around her waist. "I found him like this."

"No...no..." she sobbed, her cries enough to rend his heart in two.

Henri focused on the task at hand. "These streets are treacherous. We must summon the law."

Adrienne pressed on, determined to find the reason for the grisly scene before her. "How did you find him?"

Henri sighed. "He departed my company, perhaps to relieve himself. I came searching for him after he did not return for some thirty minutes. I fear he has been robbed. His billfold and pocket watch are missing."

"His ring?" She referenced the inscribed signet ring Andrew wore.

Henri shook his head. "I know not, Adrienne. The sheriff will deal with things now." He half-carried her out into the open, gesturing to the youth who had accompanied her from the hotel. “Boy, get the law. There’s been a murder.”

15

Sarah wept heart wrenching sobs in George's arms, as the stunned party sat in their suite. Bessie kept an arm possessively around Adrienne, as Henri paced the room. The sheriff had been summoned with great haste, and now was interviewing the madame at the brothel. Deciding it would be kinder to the ladies' delicate natures, George and Henri made the quick decision not to tell Sarah and Adrienne of Andrew's final activities. The sheriff, however, was keenly intrigued by the prospect of a prostitute committing the murder, and sped off with haste.

"How can this be? George, you promised never to leave his side!" Sarah's anguish transformed to rage, pushing her husband, and pummeling him with harmless fists.

Henri paused from across the room,

admonishing the woman. "George is hardly to blame, Madame Forrest. Andrew resisted greatly at the prospect of being followed to see to his needs."

Adrienne's hollow eyes met his, as Sarah renewed her weeping, apologizing to her husband. "I am sorry. I do not know what I will tell my father! Andrew is...was everything to him!"

Tearing his eyes away from Adrienne, Henri departed the room. His guilt and anger at the pain in Adrienne's expression paled slightly, as he saw Francine sleeping soundly through all the turmoil. Grabbing a decanter off the table in their suite, he poured a measure of whiskey, downing it with one gulp, as the door creaked open, a beam of light entering the dark orifice.

"Henri?" Adrienne's tentative, soft voice permeated his dark thoughts.

He strode to the door, slipping out into the hall. Her eyes were ringed red from shed and unshed tears. He wanted to gather her slender form to his chest, and whisper soothing words of comfort into her disheveled blonde hair. "Yes?"

"Was that...where Andrew was...a brothel?" She hesitated, the word sticking in her throat.

Henri leaned against the floral printed wall, eyes upward. "It is not proper..."

"Damn propriety!" She touched his arm, her hand cold even through his shirt. "Tell me."

His memory flashed back to Andrew, and the Creole prostitute wrapped around him. "Yes," he muttered, almost inaudibly.

Adrienne's hand left his arm, creeping up the slender column of her throat in pure shock. "But he..."

"Many men seek comfort outside their vows, Adrienne. It is nothing new." He regretted his cold words, as her face fell.

"I see." She stepped away, turning to go back to comfort her friend. "I think it best we return in the morning, at least, the Forrests and myself. I know Francine wishes to do some shopping."

"Adrienne..." Henri reached out, catching her free hand. "I am terribly sorry. To cause you anguish, well, it was the last thing I would ever wish to do."

Her body tensed and relaxed, in a fluid motion. Gazing over her shoulder, she nodded subtly, giving his hand a gentle squeeze. "I know." Then, much like a vision in the night, she was gone.

Henri spun on a heel, returning to the interior of the room. Francine was sitting up in bed, her accusatory eyes holding promises of discomfort. He was not in a mood to deal with his wife's flighty moods, as he stripped off his boots and breeches. "Not now, woman," he growled low.

"What is all this? There's so much noise in this hotel!" Francine pressed on, without heed to his request.

"Adrienne's fiancé has been found murdered, if you care. Now, I would like to get some rest, as there will probably be things to deal with in the morning." He rolled onto his side, blanking out her grunts of protest. What he did not expect were the tears. The bed shook with her cries until he sat up. "What is it? Are you ill?" She certainly could not be crying for Adrienne's loss.

"I am with child," Francine spluttered, and Henri felt his body grow cold.

"With child?" he repeated carefully. "You should have told me sooner. Taking you into the city was careless. We shall return home in the morning."

His word final, Henri laid back down. If he calculated correctly, she must have become pregnant on their wedding night. His stomach twisted. What kind of mother would the woman beside him be? He would have to strive to find a nursemaid to adequately care for the baby. Sleep never came to him that night, and the following day, he would have to face Adrienne again, all the longing and desire still fresh in his heart.

The return trip to Jefferson Parish bore none of the joyous overtones of the previous day. Adrienne had graciously helped Sarah pen an urgent telegram to her father, who would begin his journey to New Orleans as soon as his affairs were put in order. He would continue on to visit his daughter and grandson after arrangements were made for Andrew. No mention was made of Adrienne, and it was possible Andrew had not told his father yet of their engagement.

Several weeks had passed, and Adrienne still was unable to pull herself from her grief. Arnaud watched his daughter staring absently out the parlor window, and his heart ached. He knew of Andrew's proclivities for whores, but thought his daughter did not need to be aware of such things. He sighed deeply, realizing again that Francine's news of a child had pushed Adrienne's situation into the background. It might have been for the best. He slipped away, leaving her to her contemplations, a hand over the ever persistent ulcer in his stomach.

Adrienne was vaguely aware of her audience, and even if she acknowledged her father's presence, her mind was on other things. Henri's revelation of Andrew's final moments cut her to the core, and she mourned the man she knew, yet hated the one she did not. Most of all, she remembered the moment he grasped her hand in comfort, and the look in his eyes, which had indicated he wished for something more. Impossibilities upon impossibilities, she scolded herself gently for the traitorous feelings she had wished to banish with her marriage to Andrew.

"Miss?" Hetty peeked her head into the room. "There is a slave girl from St. Esprit here. She insisted on seeing you. Mama nearly clapped her on the head for rudeness."

Adrienne walked after Hetty to the kitchens, finding Sabine sitting at the table, casting suspicious glances to Helene. "Sabine! What is it? Is my sister well?"

"As well as can be, miss. She moans constantly about her pregnancy. Mama does her best to soothe her, but the slaves are feared."

"Coquettish child! Would I ever dare speak so freely!" Helene slammed a fist into her bread dough.

Sabine ignored her, beckoning Adrienne closer. "Mama wishes you to visit again. She says she can give you answers."

"Voodoo witch!" Helene cursed. "She will bring down the wrath of God on our home."

Raising her chin, Sabine's eyes held back tears. "Mama is a proud woman, Miss Helene. You would do well to treat her with respect."

"Enough." Adrienne held up her hand. "Helene, we must be kind. St. Esprit is home to Francine, and it is our duty to be hospitable."

Helene dipped her head, eyes still fiercely pinned on Sabine. "Yes, Miss Adrienne."

Adrienne gently ushered Sabine to the kitchen door. "I will call on my sister tomorrow afternoon. It is only polite I send a message first. Will you deliver it? Maybe to Monsieur Du Cormier?"

Sabine bobbed her head eagerly. "As soon as I get back, miss!"

As a mother would to her child, Adrienne straightened the lopsided apron, and fastened a loose button on the girl's dress. "Good. I will see you soon." She flashed a warm smile, before giving Sabine a soft push to be on her way.

Helene clucked her tongue disapprovingly, as Adrienne turned back into the warmth of the kitchen. "That girl's mama is bad news, Miss Adrienne. She's surely a witch, as I live and breathe!"

"Surely there is no harm in..."

Slapping the bread dough on the counter, Helene cut off her response, "Madame Clotilde is known throughout the parish, miss. A Voodoo Queen, they say. Men and women have died seeking her advice. You see. St. Esprit is cursed, miss! Best to stay away...from Monsieur Du Cormier and all them heathen worshipers!"

"Monsieur Du Cormier is a good Christian man." Adrienne hardly believed the words, but it was better than rumors abounding the plantation. "I will go see my sister tomorrow, and you will hold your tongue, Helene!"

Eyes wide with shock, Helene nodded curtly, going back to her cooking. Adrienne rushed from the kitchen, breathing heavily. She had never spoken to dear Helene like that in all her years. Pressing a hand to her breast to still her heart, she wondered what Sabine had meant about her mother having answers to her questions. Adrienne remembered Henri crouched over Andrew's body. He denied killing her fiancé, but what if he had enlisted the help of another?

Shaking off the horrible thought, Adrienne returned to the parlor, and shut the door. Returning to her chair, she was surprised to see a crumpled paper on the seat, which hadn't been there when she left the room. Her hands shook, as she lifted the missive, mouthing the words slowly.

I love her. I will do anything to have her. I will kill for her.

Adrienne dropped the paper, watching it flutter to the floor.

16

Henri watched Adrienne's carriage approaching St. Esprit's main house, dirt rising up from the drive. He shifted astride his horse, the leather saddle creaking. Fleming squinted, lifting a hand to shield his eyes, tracking Henri's gaze.

"She'll be visitin' the mistress, no doubt." He spat a stream of tobacco onto the ground, where it quickly sank into the earth.

Swiveling in his saddle, Henri scrutinized his overseer, wondering what the statement meant. He had not brought up Sabine's message to anyone, aside from Francine, who begrudgingly accepted the visit, feeling immensely sorry for herself. He made an indifferent grunt, tapping the flanks of his horse with his heels, and guiding the stallion back to the stables.

By the time he walked back into the house,

Adrienne's carriage had departed. A small traveling trunk stood upright in the entry, and Henri raised an eyebrow, stopping a passing slave. "What's this?"

"Miss Beaumont might be staying the night, Master Henri." Her eyes were wide, almost fearful at his impending reaction.

"Ah, yes, Francine will be needing support. The first months are the hardest, I'm told," he mused to no one in particular, least of all the maid carrying a basin. She performed a passable curtsey, hurrying away.

Henri rubbed the back of his neck, taking off his hat in bewilderment. He traced the familiar path to his library, finding solace in the contracts with merchants for the impending crop. He would be a rich man after harvest. Richer, Henri reminded himself. St. Esprit sat on fertile soil, so her crop was always in demand.

In irritation, Henri tossed aside his pen, slashing a line of ink over one of the contracts. He swore under his breath, blotting at the mark with his handkerchief. A knock on the door interrupted his attempts at cleaning the document. "What?" he barked, scowling at the closed portal.

Sabine deftly opened the door, balancing a tray on her hip. "Mama said you might be wanting something to eat."

Henri frowned, crumpling the kerchief and tossing it aside. "Thank you, Sabine."

The girl set the tray down on his desk with no great urgency. The silver service contained a pot of tea and some cakes artfully arranged on gold rimmed china. A spicy smell wafted from the confections, and he felt his stomach rumble in response. Before Sabine could depart, Henri stopped her.

"How is my wife?" he asked, little compassion or emotion in his voice.

"Mistress Francine is uncomfortable, if I am honest, sir. Perhaps Miss Adrienne can distract her. The mistress hardly drinks or eats, sir. We are worried for her health, and that of the babe." Sabine spoke so frankly, Henri almost forgot to blink.

"No beating around the bush," he muttered, before meeting her inquisitive stare. "Thank you. I will try to encourage her later to take some nourishment, for the sake of the child." With a nod of his head, Sabine was dismissed. She took her leave with quiet dignity.

Picking up a cake, Henri took a bite, enjoying the subtle sweetness of the spices used. He idly flicked a crumb off his desk, chewing slowly. He wondered if Francine was deliberately starving herself to rid her body of the child. He already knew her distaste for pregnancy, having complained bitterly about the changes in her body, her aching back, and fear of her perfect skin becoming marred. He endured each complaint with as good a nature as possible, assuring her it would be over soon.

Still, her waist had expanded much in the passing weeks. Henri never remembered his mother developing so quickly, but he tried to leave those matters to the women of the household. Scooping up the teacup, he enjoyed the warming brew, despite the even warmer weather outside. He deftly crumpled the marred contract. The merchant would just have to provide him with another.

Adrienne winced, wrinkling her nose as her sister let loose the meager contents of her stomach into a basin. Sabine carried it away, second nature, and Adrienne offered her sister a glass of water and a cool cloth.

"Pregnancy is a curse!" Francine gasped in overdramatic agony. "I do not know how women manage to have so many brats if they must suffer so in the ensuing months!"

Adrienne wisely held her tongue, accepting the cloth back. "It should not be like this for long. Sarah took to her bed infrequently during her time."

"Sarah is a ninny." Heaving again, Francine managed to control her treacherous stomach, curling into a ball.

"Has the doctor been?" Adrienne tried another tactic.

She scoffed. "He says it is a woman's due lot to suffer for Eve's sins! What utter..."

Sabine appeared at the exact moment. "Mistress Francine, try some ginger. Mama says..."

"I do not care! Get out, both of you. Let me suffer in silence. Draw the curtains."

The pair departed the room in silence. Adrienne turned to find her bedchamber, when Sabine's cool hand met her skin. "Mama says tonight. You must be ready." She moved off so quickly, it was as if she had never been there.

"What is tonight?" Henri's booming voice filled the now-empty corridor. "Is that why you are here? What promises has Clotilde made?"

Her palms began to sweat, and she absently brushed them on the folds of her skirt. "Nothing was promised."

He stepped towards her with purpose. "You still do not believe I had nothing to do with the death of Mr. Dixon."

"I...I do not believe you...you could be capable of such an act, no." Adrienne fought out the words, wondering if she was truly convinced by her own admission.

Henri crossed his arms over his chest. "I must ask you not to get yourself involved in such affairs, Adrienne. While Clotilde may seem to have the best of intentions, it is her interests she keeps at heart, not yours. You must know this."

"You are not my father, sir. Only he holds authority to tell me what to do." She raised her chin an inch, fire entering her cool blue eyes.

He circled her slowly, stopping before Francine's door. "That may be so, but I hold the authority in my own house, mademoiselle, and I refuse to see a guest here taken in by charlatans!"

"If you fear them so, why not sell them?" The tremor in her voice made Adrienne feel ashamed in her very question.

Henri stepped forward, until his presence surrounded her. He smelled of fresh air and warm, sun kissed skin. She bit into her lower lip, wondering if he could see her rapid pulse in the nape of her neck. "Another plantation owner might be less tolerant. Would you see Sabine beaten? Abused?"

"Yet you allow them to continue their practices. Why?" Her question came out with a breathless heave, her voice catching in her throat.

"A happy slave thinks little of rebellion, my dear." He withdrew, taking all his essence with him, and turned to place a hand on Francine's doorknob. "I can ask you, but I will not order you. Do what you must to achieve peace of mind, but take what she says with care." He entered the room, closing the door silently behind him.

Spinning on her heel, Adrienne fled, running to the opposite side of the house, and her given room for the evening. The cool air whooshed over her face, as she pulled the door open. Someone had drawn the curtains to keep out the summer heat. Next to the bed, a vase of pale pink roses filled the air with a heady aroma. Adrienne pressed a hand to her brow, reclining back on the soft sheets of the bed.

Sabine clutched Adrienne's hand, leading her towards the barn. She could hear the hum of the slaves, feet slapping the dirt floor, and the building rhythm of song. Her dress trailed, entangling around her legs, the hoops long discarded for comfort. Her hair was unbound, caressing her shoulders in blonde waves. Adrienne felt her heart rise, freedom from the confines of her gender.

The interior of the barn glowed with lantern light, Clotilde standing amongst what could be described as her congregation. The singing rose and fell in fevered pitches. Sabine brought Adrienne forward, placing her hand in her mother's, and stepping back, eyes wide. Clotilde turned her hand palm up, tracing a finger along the lines. It was a startling contrast, the caramel skin against porcelain white.

"You seek answers. Answers I can give. There is a cost. Are you here freely?" Clotilde's voice flowed along with the beat of the low hum of music.

"I am." Adrienne straightened her back, aware of the many eyes fixed on her.

Clotilde inclined her head regally. "My mother, a great woman, lived in Haiti. She was a queen in all her right. She spoke of a *loa*, a graceful, fickle creature. I have seen her summoned once in my life."

Blue eyes met brown, locking in consent to the unspoken question. "I know humans are used as...conduits for *loa*. If this will give me my answers, I agree."

Circling Adrienne, Clotilde ran her fingers through her hair. "My mother told me she was beautiful, with hair of glimmering sunlight." Someone pressed a bone cup into Adrienne's hand. "Drink."

The sweet liquor coated Adrienne's tongue. The refined alcohol made her dizzy, having never drunk anything so potent and rich before. The room around her began to spin, Clotilde's face transforming in a blur before her eyes. She swooned, and arms encompassed her.

17

Henri awoke to his door opening. Framed in the moonlight was a beauty far beyond any he had seen before. He rubbed his eyes, wondering if he could be dreaming. Laughter, tinkling like the misty rain, rose from her form. He sat up, the sheets falling away from his bare chest. The woman stepped closer, and he blinked, murmuring one word, "Adrienne?"

"A pretty name, but not mine." The creature cocked her head to the side, eyes sparkling in the dark. "You look so familiar to me. A lover?" Her hand extended out, beckoning him to her. The door shut slowly of its own volition.

Henri swung his legs out of the bed, crossing the floor to her. Blonde hair fell in her face, and he brushed it back, raising her chin. "Adrienne, wake up," he urged softly. The blue of her eyes had been blotted out by pure black.

"If you must, call me Charlotte. She came, though. I can hear her inside," the woman hissed low, leaning her cheek into his hand. "She demanded answers. I liked her immediately. Pretty little thing, full of desire."

Moving to withdraw his hand, he found it captured between the palms of the woman, whose body and appearance was entirely Adrienne, but her behavior and demeanor not. She brought his hand to her breast, and his breath caught in his throat.

"She desires you, *mon cher*."

Henri let his fingertips linger on the dress, a pale rose color, and realized this creature was speaking fluent French. He understood every word. "She...she would not want this."

"Oh, but she does. She knows now. It wasn't you who took her beloved. She knows it was an unfortunate accident." She arched her back delicately. "Take her. My gift. She wants this..." She stretched out a hand, her cool palm connecting with his chest in such a gesture, Henri felt his desire growing stronger.

"You must go."

The pout came to her full lips. "A kiss then. A parting gesture, and I shall leave this form happy."

Henri knew if he kissed this woman, Adrienne, whomever, he would come undone. Part of him knew she would not leave him in peace, if he did not. He cupped the delicate face in his hand, and she purred low, pleased by the touch. Encircling her waist with his free arm, he drew her close, lowering his lips to hers. Light seemed to explode from behind his eyes as they connected. Knowing he could go no further, Henri stepped back, withdrawing all contact. The light faded.

"Thank you," she cooed softly, and left the room.

Baffled, Henri padded slowly back to his bed, returning to the now cold sheets. He shivered, demanding his lust temper itself, but he would find little sleep that night.

Adrienne awoke the next morning, fully dressed in her bed. Someone had left her a glass of water, and she greedily gulped it down, forgetting all manners and propriety. She barely remembered the previous night, aside from being led into the barn by Sabine. Flashes of Henri entered her mind, and Adrienne clutched her head, rubbing her temples. "It was another dream," she assured herself, climbing out of the bed.

A soft rap came on her door, and she called out for the person to enter. Sabine waltzed in, a breakfast tray balanced on her hip. "Good morning, well, afternoon, Miss Adrienne."

She blanched. "Afternoon? Sabine, please tell me what happened last night. I only remember being escorted to the barn."

Sabine turned her back, setting the tray down on a table. "Nothing, miss. Mama told you Master Henri did not murder your fiancé. You swooned, and we carried you back here."

Adrienne stood, balancing herself. "I remember..."

"It can be disorienting, but Mama says it will pass." Sabine faced her, nervously biting her lip, the white teeth a stark contrast against her dark skin.

"What can be?" Adrienne stepped forward shakily, grasping Sabine by the shoulders. "What?"

Henri stepped through the open door. "Adrienne? What is going on?" He stared at the two, Adrienne's nails nearly digging into the girl's flesh with fear. He carefully dislodged her from Sabine, and dismissed her with a nod of his head. She scampered from the room.

"Adrienne, speak to me." Henri supported her with an arm around her waist. "What happened?"

She struggled away from him, tearing around the room, throwing clothing in her trunk. "I must leave. I cannot stay here. Please, convey my apologies to Francine." Her eyes darted over her face, paling at the memory of her dream. Or was it a dream? She flushed, leaning against a chair.

Henri hastened to her side, offering an arm. "Please tell me why you are upset." His voice was soothing, but urgent.

"I have to go, please. Call my carriage." She enveloped herself in her cloak, pulling away from him.

"Adrienne, did they hurt you? I do not think I could live with myself if I knew you were put in harm's way." He held her in place, embracing her lightly.

She collapsed forward, sobbing openly on his chest. "It is too much, Henri. I know you did no harm to Andrew, yet, I had strange dreams. A blonde woman beckoned me to oblivion. She presented you to me." She fisted her hand, futilely pushing at him.

Henri grew quiet, but his hold on her did not

loosen. “Adrienne, I thought it was a dream. You, or rather, a woman named Charlotte, came to me last night. She begged to...lay with me.”

Adrienne wept. “I am mad. They will lock me up, I am certain!”

He held her at arms’ length. “No. This is the work of Clotilde. We will keep this secret. Hush now. I will arrange your carriage.” He brushed back her tangled hair. “Do not fear. I did not take advantage of you.” He released her, the warmth draining from her body, and departed.

Adrienne sat on the bed, letting the remaining tears fall.

Henri stormed into the kitchens, allowing the door to slam against the wall. Everyone, aside from Clotilde, jumped and scattered, leaving the master and cook in silence. “What did you do to Adrienne? I will only have the truth, woman.”

Clotilde patiently dried her hands on her apron, rotating to face him. “I gave her answers.”

Henri pounded his fist on the table. “Damnit, woman! So help me, I will sell Sabine downriver!” He did not mean his words, and he knew she knew this as well, but a shriek from the corner had both their heads swiveling.

“No! Mama said she needed help! She knows there’s a curse. The miss, she can break the curse!”

Clotilde frowned, clamping a hand over the struggling child. “Shush!” She raised her eyes to Henri. “Yes, it is true. I used Miss Adrienne, but for the betterment of this household.”

Pointing his finger, Henri tempered his rage. "You will *never* use another family member of mine for your black magic. I will continue to permit your gatherings, but do not take advantage of my good graces again." He spun, and left the pair in the kitchen, still not satisfied his admonishment would be taken seriously.

By the time he returned to Adrienne's room, she had gone. He sat on her bed, knowing she would never willingly return to St. Esprit again.

Part II

"The mind of youth eagerly catches at
promised pleasure:
pure and innocent by nature, it thinks not
of the dangers
lurking beneath those pleasures, till too late
to avoid them."
~ *Charlotte Temple*

18

June, 1840

Adrienne leaned back in her chair, fanning herself. The summer heat fell over them like a blanket, pressing in from all sides. Her father had declined slowly in health since the birth of Francine's son, Remi. Arnaud was pleased to be a grandfather, and willing to overlook the obvious differences in the boy's appearance, compared to his father and mother. Henri had done the righteous thing, despite doubts, and claimed the child as his own, but even Adrienne could see the ache in his eyes.

The boy grew, wild and fiery, like his mother, but with an inherited sense of curiosity. Now five years of age, Remi visited Beaumont Plantation frequently, with or without the company of his mother, who had instantly handed his care over to a black nursemaid. Adrienne could see Henri struggling with parenting the boy, but he laid no blame on him. Francine had told her he vowed never to touch her again, and this pleased her greatly. He also spent weeks away from St. Esprit, taking advantage of the booming slave trade in New Orleans. When he did appear, he was gaunt, tired, and irritable. The night nearly six years ago still weighed on their minds, but they accepted it with grace, leaving it to history.

"Aunt! I found a bug!" Remi rushed into the parlor, holding out the squirming beetle.

Adrienne inspected the insect, never one to shy away from creatures. "Interesting. Should we get a jar, and find out what it is?"

Remi nodded, rushing off to the kitchen before Adrienne could rise. Helene's screams resounded through the home, and she stifled a laugh. Remi returned, the beetle contained in a jam jar. He rushed to the thick books on his grandfather's shelf, his face a mask of confusion.

"Aunt, which one is the book about bugs?"

Adrienne helped her nephew find the appropriate volume, stroking his mousy brown hair. The color sparked a memory, but no face came to mind. Arnaud limped into the room, his weight supported by a wooden cane.

"What do we have here?" He peered into the jar. "Ah, *Dynastes tityus*, commonly known as a Hercules beetle. Clever find, my boy."

Adrienne smiled at her father, loving his never-ending supply of knowledge. She turned to the page, showing Remi a sketch of the creature. "Pests."

Arnaud lowered himself into his chair. "Yes, *ma petite*. Certainly, a pest."

"Why, Grandpa?" Remi studied his find.

"They eat wood. Best to squash it." Arnaud wiggled his eyebrows.

Remi clung to the jar. "No! I will make him a pet."

Adrienne smiled at their interaction, knowing the previous years had been hard on him. Neighboring Texas had suffered greatly, fighting independence from Mexico. They had become a republic, or so she gleaned from cryptic dinner conversations between her father and Henri. The thought of war strained Arnaud's delicate constitution, and he feared conflict would trickle into Louisiana. Thankfully, it did not, but strings of refugees, fearing war, had trailed into the state.

Watching her father carefully, Adrienne noticed him wince in pain slightly, but he hid it well from the boy. She smiled sympathetically, knowing he had often concealed his pain from her. Now, there was little doubt her father was dying. The doctors murmured about his ulcer having grown cancerous, a word that blackened households everywhere. They tried to hide the grim diagnosis from ladylike ears, but Adrienne was no fool. Her goal now was to make her father's final time on the earth worthwhile.

"I do not think he will last long in the jar, Remi. Perhaps we should release him in the woods, hmm?" Arnaud questioned the boy, whose brow furrowed thoughtfully.

Finally, after little prompting, Remi agreed, and tugged on his grandfather's hand. "Come on! I need help!"

Adrienne stood quickly. "Remi, your grandfather needs his rest. Here, I will come help release your beetle." She held out her hand, and the child grasped it.

"Bye, Grandfather!" Remi waved as the pair left the room, Adrienne bestowing an understanding smile on her father, who looked distressed by his inability to join in the antics.

Adrienne paused, leaning down and whispering to Remi. He popped his head up, and grinned at his grandfather. "I'll come back and tell you about it!" This brought a genuine happiness to the old man's face, and they departed for the edge of the plantation.

Henri reigned his horse by the familiar tree, where he had encountered Adrienne alone that day, all those years ago. He watched as she walked, hand in hand, with his son. Removing his hat, Henri rubbed the back of his neck, urging the doubt that crept up in his mind to return to blessed ignorance. Deciding to not interrupt the tender moment between aunt and nephew, he rode up to the house, handing off the reins to a slave.

Stamping his feet to rid his boots of dust, Henri entered, needing no announcement. He wove his way to the familiar study, knocking on the door. When no answer came from within, Henri quietly turned the handle. The room was silent, yet a lingering cloud of uncertainty crept up into his chest. He surveyed his surroundings quickly, eyes landing on his worst fear. Arnaud was slumped in his armchair.

Rushing to the door, Henri shouted out for help, and ran to the man, kneeling by his side. He was still breathing, but barely. A few men hurried into the room. Henri gruffly ordered one to fetch a doctor, and he tenderly hoisted the old man with the help of the remaining slave. They carefully bore their burden up to his bedchamber, where a maid joined them, to make the master comfortable.

Seeing that his father-in-law was in good hands for the moment, Henri ran down the stairs, taking them two at a time. He burst out into the yard, and sprinted over to Adrienne and Remi. His son looked up in confusion, and Adrienne reached out to steady him.

"Adrienne...you must come. Your father..." He did not need to utter another word. Adrienne picked up her skirts, and made haste in the direction of the house.

Remi tilted his head, studying his parent curiously. "Papa, what is happening?"

Henri lifted the boy, and began a slow trek to the house. "Your grandfather is very ill. We must fetch your mother, and return to be by his side."

Nodding solemnly, Remi looped his arms around Henri's neck, holding tightly as they approached the stables. He stepped back, as a man on a strong stallion galloped from them, in the direction of the town, to fetch the doctor. Addressing the remaining stable hand, he requested his horse, seating Remi in the saddle in front of him. He rode off to St. Esprit at a steady gallop, listening to Remi chortle with joy at the bouncy ride.

Upon arrival to the plantation, Remi was swiftly

passed off to his nursemaid, and Henri went in search of his errant wife. On his trek, he ordered the carriage prepared. Eventually, he found his wife in a darkened room, suffering from one of her migraines.

"Francine, we must go to Beaumont. Your father collapsed," he stated into the shadowy room.

She half-heartedly groaned, tossing an arm out. "Is the old man really dying this time? If not, I cannot be bothered to move. This heat is utterly oppressive."

Henri could hardly suppress his anger at her flippant disregard for her father's well-being. "Wife, you will rise from your bed, and prepare yourself. I am too often capitulating to your whims, but in this instance, I refuse. You are required at your father's bedside, and I will bear no excuse to your distraught sister!"

Francine lifted her head. "My distraught sister? The one you long to have in your bed? Yes, Henri, I know you still pine for her after all these years. It matters not if I am there. I will inherit all of Beaumont when that man dies, and I will make her destitute. How will she appeal to you then?"

Refraining from removing her from the bed, tossing her over his shoulder, and forcing her into the carriage, Henri attempted reason. "Deathbed changes to wills are more common than you think, my dear. Should you not show face, your father may disinherit you. Where will Remi be then? I am hardly going to give a child not of my blood St. Esprit."

Bolting up, she squinted at him. "You have no proof."

“Do I? Your statement there is enough to hold the doubt I have in my mind.” Henri was crushed, his worse fears confirmed by his own wit.

Francine swung her legs over the bed. “It matters not. I shall leave Beaumont to Remi.” She pushed past him, hollering for Sabine and her cloak, putting on the most tragic of airs.

“We shall see, madame. We shall see.”

19

Arnaud's rasping breath permeated the solemn mood of those surrounding the noble man's deathbed. The doctor spoke quietly with Henri in the corner of the room, shaking his head when asked if Arnaud had much time. Adrienne perched on the edge of the bed, holding her father's hand. He seemed to have aged drastically, hollow crevices under his once vibrant eyes. His skin was sallow and lined. She wiped back a tear, continuing to stroke her beloved parent's hand.

Adrienne remembered asking her father once about their mother's death. He said she slowly slipped into sleep, never waking again. She almost wished the same for her father, but she so desired to share a final word with him. Adrienne lifted her head, feeling Henri's eyes on her. His expression was dire, and she knew she might not have those moments. Her chest heaved, and she cried anew.

"*Petite*..." The familiar nickname emerged from her father's dried lips. Immediately, everyone crowded around, Francine shoving her way to the other side. However, Arnaud only had eyes for Adrienne.

"I need to speak with Henri."

Francine opened her mouth to protest, but Adrienne silenced her. "We will get something to eat. I'm sure Helene has some stew simmering." She stood, and gracefully departed the room. Francine had no choice but to follow, and express her outrage once they were out of earshot.

"You! Always his favorite! Well, I tell you this, when he dies, and he will die, I will have Beaumont, and you can live with the slaves!"

Adrienne shook, knowing her words were true. Although, Bessie would never see her destitute, as they had discussed on many an occasion. Adrienne would always be welcome at Belle Rivière. She refused to take on her sister's ravings at a time like this, but when the claw-like fingers encircled her arm, she turned and slapped Francine with all her might.

"You may throw me out of the home I have known and loved, but you will never touch me again!"

Francine stood in shock before launching herself forward, grasping Adrienne by the hair. Her screams had slaves emerging from all corners of the house, watching their beloved mistress struggle against her sister. Henri threw open the door, and wrenched his wife away from Adrienne, holding her in an iron grip. He knew who had instigated the fray.

"Madame! You behave abhorrently! I am ashamed." Henri released Francine, spinning her away from Adrienne. Not wanting to remain to face more wrath, Adrienne fled down the stairs, her sobs heard through the house. Many withdrew, leaving the man to scold his errant wife.

Helene's arms opened instinctively to receive Adrienne. She hushed her, humming a soft lullaby. When Adrienne finally composed herself, Helene held her at arms' length, brushing away the tears. "Now, now, child. We all know Master Arnaud would never leave you bereft. Sit, and have something to eat."

Lowering herself into a chair, Adrienne raised her eyes, seeing Sabine at the table for the first time. She had blossomed in five years, growing from innocent child to worldly woman. Her eyes still haunted Adrienne, who focused on picking at the slice of bread set before her.

"Why are you here?" Adrienne asked, finally, lifting her eyes to meet Sabine's.

Sabine straightened in the chair. "I go everywhere with Mistress Francine. It is expected." The lyrical tone to her voice had not left.

Strange dreams had haunted Adrienne since the night she sought answers about Andrew's murder. A woman in a white dress, with shimmering blonde hair lifted by an invisible breeze, often came to her, demanding payment for tasks done. No matter how many times she professed ignorance, the woman insisted. The result was Adrienne waking suddenly, gasping for breath and drenched in a cold sweat.

"Mama says she still needs you."

Helene squared her shoulders. "Now, none of

that, girl! We've had many a misfortune in this house since your mama took an interest in our Adrienne. You just keep away! Shoo! Wait for your mistress on the porch." She swatted at Sabine, who hurried to the door.

"Not Mama, miss. *Her*." Sabine fled, before Helene could take the broom to her backside.

Adrienne lowered her head, leaving her bread untouched. "I best get back to Papa." She moved away from the table, but Helene stopped her.

"Miss Adrienne, it's not my place, but what did you promise Clotilde? Many a person has promised more than they know to her in exchange for knowledge."

Anger seeped into her body, but once she saw Helene's concerned expression, Adrienne softened. "I promised nothing I know of."

Helene caressed her cheek. "You may have given her more than you should have. Please, for our family, stay away from Clotilde. She only thinks of her own benefit."

Taking the old cook's hand in both of hers, Adrienne brushed a kiss over her weathered cheek. "I have no desire to encounter her again. My dreams have been troubled since then. I must get back to Papa."

Helene released her, turning back to her stove. Out of the corner of her eye, she caught a glimpse of Sabine, running off the porch. Crossing herself, Helene lifted the wooden spoon, and slowly stirred the stew.

The study was quiet when he entered, preparing to complete a task given to him by a dying man. Henri hesitated, holding the official document in his trembling hands. What he was about to do, if discovered, would most likely end in a prison sentence, with all his assets seized. Flourishing the ink pen, he scored out the portion of the will declaring Francine the sole heir, and replacing it with Adrienne's name. The reasoning for the addendum flowed from the tip of the pen, stating Francine's marriage had provided her with suitable means, whereas Adrienne was left bereft of proper care.

Setting aside a hefty purse for the official who would eventually be coming to verify the will, he knew he had the upper hand on the man. The fat lawyer had a taste for women, and one night in New Orleans, he had gone too far, killing one. Henri just so happened to witness the event. It was convenient how his wicked past had come back to help him in his now prosperous future.

Returning the document to the leather wallet, Henri leaned back in his chair. With a stroke of his pen, he had made Adrienne Beaumont quite wealthy. Still young and beautiful, she would quickly have a rush of suitors, pleading for her hand. He ground his teeth, hating the very thought. If Adrienne had been a beauty in her younger years, age had only enhanced every feature. Now twenty-two years of age, she would command a room upon entry, even though she now would adorn herself in black garments, forever respectful of southern traditions of mourning.

Five grueling years had passed since he had first

laid eyes on Adrienne at the ball where he would seal his fate. Pulling a cigar from the drawer, he struck a match and lit it, breathing out rings of smoke. What he wouldn't give to change his stars that very night. If he had only known, not craved standing, Adrienne might be at his side now. She might be sitting in a chair, legs curled under her skirts, reading a novel, while tendrils of blonde escaped to caress her neck.

"Our children would be legitimate, that's for one," Henri muttered, his teeth clamped down on the end of the cigar.

Henri traced a finger over the embossed leather. Adrienne only had the vaguest idea of how to truly a plantation, despite her father's earlier confidences in her business abilities. He resolved to offer his services to help her get Beaumont Plantation back up to its former glory. She would object, ever unwilling to impose on his good nature, but he would insist. Contemplating the end of his cigar, Henri made himself a dark promise. If he could not have Adrienne as lawful wife, he would have her any way he could.

20

A summer storm blew in on the day of Arnaud's funeral. Black clothed figures entered the small church, to pay their final respects to a kind man many had known, and loved, in the Parish. Adrienne greeted every one, sharing whispered words of comfort with all. Henri admired her from afar, still ashamed his own wife had feigned illness to avoid the mourning. Remi stood at his side, clutching his hand in a small, black suit. Despite Francine's vocal protests, the boy would say goodbye to the only grandparent he knew.

Miraculously, Francine stated she would see to the reading of the will after the funeral. Shameless hussy. She would be in for a mighty shock. He smiled inwardly at his deception, and reveled in the knowledge of how close he would grow to Adrienne, gradually breaking down her barriers, until she fell into his arms. He deserved happiness, and that kiss still burned in his memory.

Remi slipped away, going to stand next to Adrienne, and offer childlike comfort. Guilt panged Henri, and he felt a strange sort of pity for the boy, who would one day find out he was not the wealthy heir to a plantation. Still, he doubted Adrienne would see him destitute. As the mourners departed, he nodded his head to several with whom he had done business. Then, he made his way over to Adrienne.

"We should go soon," he whispered, surprised when she shook her head.

Her blue eyes, rimmed with tears, met his. "We must accompany Papa to his final resting place."

Henri nodded with understanding, cursing his insensitivity. He had wanted to see Adrienne's face so desperately when she found out she owned Beaumont, he forgot the cemetery. "Apologies. I will see to the carriage."

Adrienne's hand found his sleeve. "Francine is not coming, is she?"

Henri shook his head, his irritation rising anew. "No, she is not. We will bid him farewell in her stead."

Her hand remained. "It is a shame. I would have thought there would be at least a shred of kindness in her icy heart. I am sorry, Henri. You do not deserve this."

Henri covered her hand with his, giving it a gentle squeeze. "We all make our choices, Adrienne." He gazed down at Remi, watching the unfamiliar crowds. "I made mine with youthful ignorance. I am sorry as well." He ushered the boy away, resolving not to fault him further for the sins of his mother.

As he approached the wagon containing Arnaud's coffin, Henri glanced back once at Adrienne, poised and pale. He admired her strength, as he had from the first moment. His feelings of love burned anew. He should be at her side, giving full support. Francine should be a spinster, or dead. He shook his head at the dark thoughts, something he thought he had banished many years prior. Thoughts of Clotilde, and her rituals, permeated his mind for an instant, and he jumped as Sabine mysteriously appeared at his side, as if on cue.

"Girl, you would do well to explain your purpose here," Henri growled, still not forgetting the role she played on that fateful night.

Sabine curtseyed. "My mistress requested to know how things were progressing."

"Well, now get."

She did not listen, and instead, inched closer. "She can help, you know."

Henri lifted his hand. "Move now, girl, or find yourself at the end of a whip."

She never faltered, despite the threats. "She can make it better. Perhaps even find you happiness with Miss Adrienne."

"You speak out of turn." Henri glared at Sabine, until she withdrew. How could such a shy child turn into a mischievous, meddling woman? He had no doubt it was her mother's influence, yet Benji had warned him not to trifle with Clotilde. He was convinced she had caused the downfall of their last master.

Adrienne, with lowered head, joined them shortly after Sabine's departure, and the trio followed the wagon to lay Arnaud next to his Marie.

Francine was sitting in the study, when Henri and Adrienne arrived back to Beaumont. Adrienne removed her black bonnet, revealing perfectly coifed hair. She had taken care with her appearance for the funeral, not wanting to have her last moments with her father as a broken woman. She passed it to Hetty, who left the room. The attorney sat at the desk, going through the legal documents.

"Thank you all for gathering here, and I must express my deepest condolences. Monsieur Beaumont was a kind, gracious man." He perched his wire-rimmed spectacles on the end of his narrow nose, peering out at the assembled people.

Adrienne lowered her chin, bringing the lace handkerchief to her eyes. "Thank you, Monsieur Dellacorte. We appreciate your sentiments." The rustling of papers sent her gaze upward again, and she watched him withdraw the written will. Her heart thumped, knowing what was to come. She had made arrangements with Bessie to stay at their home, her bags already packed upstairs.

Monsieur Dellacorte cleared his throat. "I, Arnaud Beaumont, being in sound mind and body, leave Beaumont Plantation and all its holdings, property, and slaves to my daughter..."

Adrienne felt Francine lean forward in the chair, her knuckles whitening on the armrests. She could have sworn her sister stopped breathing for a moment. When the name came, it took Adrienne a moment to register what had been said.

"...to my daughter, Adrienne Beaumont."

Francine, also shocked by the revelation, squeaked with indignation. "What? That cannot be right! Give it here, old man." She stood, snatching the paper from his hand, scanning it. "What is this? My name has been scored out! Who did this? You?" She pointed at Monsieur Dellacorte.

Grabbing his wife, and forcing her back into the chair, Henri growled, "What do you care, woman? You have all you could want!"

Adrienne lifted her hands. "Please...on this day of mourning, must we have strife?" She turned her head to Monsieur Dellacorte. "Sir, when was this change made?" She made careful note of the fleeting glance between Henri and the nervous lawyer. "Sir? Surely there must be some date noted on the addendum?"

"I...I do not see any such note," the man bumbled, shuffling more paperwork.

Pressing her lips together, Adrienne rose, delicately excusing herself from the room. She crossed the entryway, taking in the many features of her childhood home. Doubt swam in her already troubled mind. The door to the study slammed, and she jumped in time to see a vengeful Francine stalking toward her.

"You! What did you do?" she screeched, drawing slaves from around the house to the site of the confrontation, peeking around doors and statues.

Adrienne straightened her back. "Francine, control yourself. I do not know what possesses you to behave in such an unladylike manner. Our father is dead. Would it be too much to ask for you to kindly act less like a spoiled child?" Francine snarled and advanced on Adrienne, who held up her hands. "And, as it seems this is now my home, I ask you to leave."

Mouth agape, Francine stopped in her tracks. She cautiously peered around at all the people she had tormented over the years; mindless slaves in her eyes. Each stared back in a manner they would have never dared to do when she lived in the home. She jabbed a finger forward. "You will regret this, Adrienne. I do not know what black magic you have wielded against our father, but it will come to haunt you!" She stormed out, and Adrienne sagged in obvious relief.

Henri strode out of the study, followed by Dellacorte. Adrienne nodded her head, and the unexpected audience flittered off to other parts of the house. She raised her chin and addressed Henri. "Sir, I do not believe you fully understand what you have wrought."

He motioned for Dellacorte to exit. As soon as he was out of sight, Henri grasped the errant chin. "You, mademoiselle, are set for life. Francine would have destroyed your home. Don't you see? Besides, I did not do it for your sake. It was the dying wish of your father."

She shook her head, pacing restlessly. "I do not care! I would have rather lived out my days in quiet tranquility! Bessie offered me that, and more! We would have been happy as old maids."

Henri laughed, spinning her to face him. "Do you not see the idiocy of that, Adrienne? You are meant for so much more. Let me help you bring Beaumont back to its former glory. Together, we can make her rise as the envy of the Parish."

Adrienne stared into his smoldering eyes, and shivered. The room seemed to shrink around them. "I..."

He dipped his head, murmuring for her ears alone. "I still care deeply for you. My desire for you has not diminished over the preceding years. If this is the only way I can be close to you, so be it. Accept my help, Adrienne. In your father's memory, if nothing else."

Her very voice betrayed her. "Yes, Henri. I will allow this, and nothing else. Make no mistake, I will not be your mistress." Memories sparked of his lips on hers, and she took a step back to preserve her modesty.

Placing space between them did little to prevent Henri from running the backs of his fingers over her cheek. "It pains me to see you so melancholy. I wish I could do something to alleviate your sadness."

"My father was a good man, sir. It will be some time before I can smile within these walls."

Henri bowed his head, and turned to go, murmuring softly back to her. "I will make it my very mission to see those eyes light up in joy and pleasure."

She opened her mouth to reply, but the closing of the front door met her shocked expression. Sitting at the foot of the stairs, Adrienne cried bitterly, as repressed emotions came bubbling forth anew.

21

Francine threw everything she could get her hands on around her bedroom, sending slaves running in fear of their mistress. The only one who remained steadfast, standing outside the chaos, was Sabine. Her mother had told her Francine would be her own undoing. She waited patiently for the woman to exhaust herself. When she finally collapsed on the bed in angry sobs, Sabine entered the room, carefully picking up shards of porcelain, and scattered clothing and jewelry.

Underneath the window, a glint of gold caught her eye. She glanced over her shoulder, before plucking the signet ring from the wooden floor. An A and D were intertwined, inscribed into the flattened gold. She sucked in a breath through her teeth, deftly slipping it into her pocket. Her mother would find this very interesting.

"Mistress Francine, shall I bring you some tea, and a cool cloth?"

Weakened by her outburst, Francine nodded, before suddenly vomiting into a basin by her bed. She glared at Sabine. "Say nothing, girl. When the time comes, you will take the babe to a family. My sins will be evident, but I do what I do to get revenge on your master."

Sabine's eyes widened, and she bobbed her head obediently, racing from the room to the kitchens. "Mother!"

Clotilde clamped a hand over her daughter's mouth. "Silence. I am aware. She asked me for a cure to her problem weeks ago. I said it was too dangerous."

"You knew?" Sabine shook her apron into the dustbin, removing the ring from her pocket. "And this?"

"A means to an end. I have a great many connections in New Orleans." Clotilde took the ring, turning it in her hand. "I convinced Francine that Adrienne would inherit the plantation if she were married. Andrew Dixon was a necessary casualty, my dear."

Sabine gasped. "Mama, if Master Henri were to find out..."

"He will not." Clotilde pinched Sabine's face in her hand. "All will fall into place, now that Miss Adrienne has Beaumont. Master Henri will go to her, and they will be unable to keep from their desires any longer. The *loa* have promised. Is the bag still in place?"

Wincing, Sabine did her best to answer in the affirmative. "But the baby?"

"Is not Master Henri's? Yes, but nor is it that of any white man."

"She hates slaves, Mama! How...?"

Clotilde raised a finger to her lips. "Sabine, you must trust the spirits. You must trust your mother. I will always guide you to a better life. One day, we will escape this, and go to the North. I will be revered, and you will be admired."

Sabine remained wordless, but her conscience screamed violently. The spirits would not want so much blood on their hands, she was sure of it. Yet, she trusted and loved her mother above all. Watching her go back to work, Sabine picked a lingering piece of porcelain from her apron, slicing her finger. She sucked on the wound tasting the coppery liquid. Visions of death fluttered before her eyes, and the Baron would laugh at the sacrifices made in his name.

Henri breathed in the morning air, having left St. Esprit early to avoid Francine. His efforts were in vain, because she had ensconced herself in her room since their return the previous day. No doubt she was mourning her loss of standing, but he was celebrating his victory. Waving off the stable boy, Henri saddled his own horse, soothing the tall stallion with strokes along his neck.

"It is disgusting, Isaac!"

Henri rubbed his head. Surely his mind was playing tricks on him.

"You open your legs for evil intent, Francine. If I had means, I would take Remi from this place. Do you know how it feels to watch your son being raised by another man?" The voice of his overseer trickled through the slats of the barn.

"Drown the whelp! I care not."

"You are a vile bitch. I don't know why I cared for you, or fell for your sobbing charms." Fleming departed, and Henri watched his shadow recede. Francine let out a cry of selfish upset, and stormed to the house.

Did she intend to kill Remi? No, not possible, yet, she no longer had purpose for him, since Beaumont now belonged to Adrienne. Henri shook his head, all his suspicions confirmed. He should confront Fleming, but he knew he had little to do with the deception. Instead, he decided he would ask Adrienne to shelter the boy. She did love Remi, despite his obvious illegitimacy.

Upon arriving at Beaumont, Henri was directed to Adrienne's location in the formidable study. He found her there, hunched over the desk, head buried in her hands.

"Oh, Adrienne. You must not grieve so. Arnaud saw great promise in you." He was at her side in an instant, lifting the stricken face to his view.

"I apologize, Henri. I never wished anyone to see me in such grief." She wiped the tears away. "You are prompt. I did not expect you."

He rose to his full height, drawing over a chair by her side. "It was best to get an idea of what we have to work with. Do you have the records?"

She passed him the leather bound ledger. "I...I cannot make sense of it. I saw my father's handwriting, and...my composure failed."

Henri smiled sympathetically. She looked as if

she had slept in the study, comforted by the unseen presence of her parents. He opened the ledger, catching sight of the portrait on the wall. The woman was so like Adrienne, and he had often remarked to Arnaud on the likeness between Adrienne and her mother. However, there was a fire, he had said, present in Adrienne, pushed back by the need to be a proper Southern lady.

"Your father was meticulous in his record keeping, Adrienne. We should be able to cut any unnecessary expenses in no time." He looked up at her, reaching out and brushing back a curl fallen from her so carefully arranged hairstyle. "Have you eaten today?" She indicated in the negative, and he stood. "You must have something, Adrienne. Come." Caring little for protocol, he wrapped his arm around her narrow waist, and escorted her to the kitchen. She was too weak to protest.

Helene stared in horror as the couple entered her domain, but sobered as she saw the state of her young charge. "I am so sorry, sir! She would not let anyone near, no sir!"

Henri lowered her into the chair, facing the fretting cook. "Some soup, maybe? She is weak." He joined her at the table, taking her slender hand in his. "Adrienne, I must ask a delicate charge of you. Perhaps it will help you heal."

Her eyes met his, and he cursed as he noted the dark circles. "Yes?"

"Remi...I fear he is in danger at St. Esprit. I would like your permission to house him here, until I can assure his safety." He sat back as Helene served Adrienne some warm broth and a slice of thick bread. He declined any food for himself.

Adrienne tentatively sipped the broth. "I do love Remi. He is a kind boy, undeserving of any ill will. Won't Francine object?"

"I doubt she knows he exists," he lamented, realizing they were not alone in the room. "I will tell her it will be better for Remi to be here. She will not dare deny me."

Adrienne frowned, stirring her broth. "If it will not cause issue, I will take on Remi."

Henri smiled, placing a reassuring hand on her shoulder. "This pleases me greatly. I will speak to his nanny, and have them moved in promptly."

"And silently, please, Henri. I wish not to confront my sister in this matter at all."

He made the promise, rising and returning to the study, to allow Adrienne peace to eat. Picking up the ledger, Henri knew the plantation was in dire straits. He penned a note on a scrap of paper, planning to wire his lawyer for funds to keep Beaumont thriving until he could make them self-sufficient. Snapping the book closed, he slipped it away in a drawer, determined to return to St. Esprit, and liberate his son from the scheming bitch.

22

Remi settled in well at Beaumont, happy to be in the company of a dear aunt, and his doting father. She chased away his nightmares, and made sure he never went without a kind word or soft kiss each day. It was a blissful existence for the young boy, so unused to having affection in his short life. Henri silently brooded at the change in his son...the boy. This was his most desired fantasy; to have a child with Adrienne, and live in familial bliss. However, it hung precariously over his head—the silent truth.

Henri made it his duty to attend to all the accounts, even though Adrienne desperately wanted to learn how to manage the plantation on her own. One evening, as the fire crackled, she leaned over the books, carefully listening to Henri's patient explanations. His watched her gentle breathing, the soft fabric of her dress brushing his thigh. Her hair had come loose from romping in the garden with Remi, and she carried the fresh scent of sun kissed skin.

"I see. Papa was too lenient with his merchant connections, affording them gross cuts when it came to the cost of the crops. He was kind to a fault." She turned her head, catching sight of him watching her. She straightened, stepping back, and lowering her eyes.

"Adrienne..." he murmured, grasping her hand in desperation. "You must..."

She stared at him pleadingly, lines creasing between her shapely brows. "I do. I truly do. You have been so unnecessarily kind to me."

Henri rose, taking her other hand. "Must we continue this charade? We are both sorely unhappy with our situations..."

She opened her mouth to protest, but closed it, knowing he spoke the truth. She waited for him to continue.

"I should have been a stronger man, in so many cases. I should have disregarded my pride. I craved nobility so much."

Shaking her head, with the faint trace of a smile, she looked up at him. "My family hardly could have brought you that. The French monarchy fell many years before I was born. There must have been more..."

He ran his thumbs tantalizingly over the backs of her hands. "Yes, but you will loathe me for it."

Face softening, Adrienne did not pull away, and he felt encouraged by her faith in him. "I grew up poor, sickeningly so. My father was a drunk, beating my mother and me for our every fault, seen and unseen. I was determined to escape such a hell. I fled, got a position as a lowly cabin boy on a ship bound for lands unknown."

Adrienne slowly led him over to one of the suites, and sat, motioning for him to do the same. He continued on with his sad epic. "Yet, it was not to be, this world of adventure. I worked the docks, hard, watching ships roll in and out."

"You told my father you inherited your money from an uncle. Is this true?"

Her memory was admirable, and Henri nodded his head. "Yes, by fortune's chance I was found by a solicitor from England. He was searching for a boy known to work on the docks. By this time, I was no longer a stringy child, but a hardened man. He gave me my father's name, and I readily identified myself."

"What had happened to your father?"

Henri's face hardened. "He...murdered my mother in a fit of unfounded jealous rage."

Her hand tightened around his, sympathy for his younger self emanating from her kind eyes. "Oh, that is truly tragic. Despite circumstances, they were your parents."

"I suppose it is true, even though they never showed much affection."

Adrienne breathed deeply. "Is that why you care so much for Remi, even though..." She stopped herself, gazing away.

He drew her back, cupping her blushing cheek. "Even what, Adrienne? I always knew you were clever. Please tell me you are not blind to the truth." A single tear slipped free, and Henri brushed it away. "It is only damaging to my pride and honor, what little I have in this moment."

"I think it takes more pride and honor to take a child under your wing, despite all his mother's...proclivities."

Henri rose, pacing in front of her. "And you? Would you feel the same if your husband brought in another child to live under your roof?"

"I...I truly do not know." He watched the uncertainty cross her face.

"And what about Andrew? Did you care for him?" All his questions bubbled forth, without rhyme or reason.

Adrienne turned her head, flushing. "I did not love him. It is true. He could never have had my heart completely. We would have lived amicably, but it would have never been love."

Henri dropped to one knee next to her. "Adrienne, I must ask you something."

She visibly trembled, fearing and desiring his question at the same time. "Henri, no. Society..."

"Damn social constraints. Do you love me?"

"Desperately." The answer came as a breathless whisper, so soft he barely heard it.

He returned to her side, caressing her face between his hands, murmuring words of comfort. He felt devilish for all his evil thoughts. The woman before him loved him, unconditionally, despite flaws and past deeds. Despite his feelings towards Remi. She loved him. Placing a finger under her chin, Henri lifted her watery blue eyes to his.

"Adrienne, I love you. I have since the moment you swept into the ballroom in that tantalizing blue confection. I am afraid I will be unable to stop loving you." He dipped his head, capturing her quivering lips with his. She resisted momentarily, but then, all walls fell, and she clung to him with wild hunger and abandon.

Stilling her, Adrienne stared at him with a quizzical expression. Henri quickly reassured her. "I know you are untouched. I would not force you. Nor would I ravish you in your father's study."

Her face a mask of understanding, she stood in a rustle of silk, and extended her hand to him, sealing her fate.

Ignoring every sensibility, Adrienne led the man she loved to her bedchamber. The house was silent, many of the slaves having retired for the evening. Her bed was turned down, and the window open, allowing in a soft breeze that rippled the curtains ever so slightly. Henri twisted the lock in the door, facing her with adoration. She went to him willingly.

His fingers deftly unhooked the line of buttons down the front of her dress, pushing it back over her shoulders, and down to her waist. She helped him remove the garment, leaving her in her petticoat and corset. Adrienne shivered as his lips found her neck and collarbone. His ever industrious fingers worked the laces of her corset and petticoat, letting them fall to the floor unheeded. He lifted her slim form from the pile of garments, clothed only in a chemise and stockings.

Unburdened of her mourning gown, Adrienne came alive, clinging to him and drawing his mouth to hers. Smiling, Henri set her down again, his hands moving to her hair. He withdrew a pin at a time until it fell in blonde waves down her slender back. Her head fell back as his hands came over her, teasing her breasts through the chemise. He lowered his mouth to her nipples, teasing them into hardened peaks beneath the thin fabric.

Henri clung to her body as she moaned softly, enjoying intimate male attention for the first time. Something unleashed inside her, and she tore at his shirt and coat, needing to have his bare skin under her hands. He willingly obliged, groaning low as her fingers explored his chest and stomach, dipping lower.

"Brave one," he murmured, capturing her lips again, and scooping her up. He bore her down on the bed. "I hope you have another."

She barely had to ask before he rent the chemise in two, revealing her bare body to his gaze. He toyed with the tops of her stockings, teasing her inner thighs in such a tantalizing manner, she felt her body bend to his will. Henri rolled them down her legs. "I would have you this way always. Nothing between your beautiful form and my touch."

Adrienne pushed back all thoughts of resistance, focusing on his lips tracing hot lines along her skin. When he lightly blew on her center, she bucked unintentionally, whimpering low. With a single finger, he traced along her damp blonde curls. She was so sensual; unlike any woman he had ever touched. Her nails left half-moon grooves in his shoulders.

"Too eager, my love. Let me pleasure you."

Adrienne's head spun, and she saw stars as he inserted a finger in her most intimate area. Henri felt himself grow rock hard, feeling her tight warmth. It was too much, and he divested himself of his breeches. Her fingertips gently brushed against his rock hard member, and he grasped them.

"Oh, my sweet. You will undo me." Henri kissed her sensually, drawing her tongue out to play chase with his as he continued to explore, until he could bear it no longer and had to possess her. "It will hurt, but I will be gentle." He positioned himself to enter her inviting body.

Adrienne gasped at the intrusion to her most intimate area. He stretched her slowly, and she felt tears prick the back of her eyes as with one final thrust, he made her a woman. There was a brief stabbing pain, but it was quickly surpassed by waves of rich pleasure as he made love to her. The stars returned and burst in bright lights as Adrienne's body arched, and Henri reached his own pinnacle. He collapsed in sheer bliss, gathering her close to his chest. As they slipped into sleep, both swore they heard the tinkling laughter of a woman.

The morning sun trickled in through the window, and Henri opened his eyes, feeling more at ease than he had been in many years. Next to him, encircled in his arms, was Adrienne, her face a mask of tranquility. He kissed her soft lips until she stirred, languid eyes meeting his. He searched them desperately for a hint of regret, and when he found none, he drew her closer, feeling her pert breasts pressing into his chest.

Skimming a hand down her thigh, Henri hooked

her leg up, arching her hips and drawing her on top of him. Adrienne's hair fell around her breasts, and she straddled his lap, waiting for his tutorial. He guided her down on him, groaning as she encompassed his manhood. Under his guidance, she rode him, picking up the rhythm easily, and finding her sweet release as he pressed his thumb to her hidden nub. She collapsed forward, and he ran his hands over her smooth back.

Adrienne's breath was hot on his neck, her words coming easily. "I love you."

Henri embraced her fiercely. "And I, you." He rolled her into the crook of his arm, staring down at the rosy cheeked face.

"Henri, did you hear...something last night?"

He etched a finger around a pink nipple. "I thought it was you, my pet."

She shook her head. "No. Was someone...in the room?" Her expression transformed to horrified.

Henri pulled her into his strong embrace, kissing her brow. "No, my love. We were alone."

"You should go to a guest room, Henri. Hetty will be up soon," she sighed softly, not wanting to relinquish him, as she clung to his shoulders.

Reluctantly releasing her, Henri swung his legs over the side of the bed. "You are right. One day, though, I will refuse to scurry off at the fear of a chambermaid encountering us."

Her lips found his shoulder and the back of his neck, as she embraced him from behind.

"Damn it, woman. Do not tempt me back to your amorous arms. Although, I would gladly keep you abed all day." He pulled on his breeches and boots, retrieving his shirt. When he looked back, she had the sheets gathered about her body.

"I will have to..." She blushed. "Blood."

Henri reached over and cupped her cheek. "Hetty will not suspect, my love. Monthly courses, no?"

Her shocked expression made him laugh heartily, and she hushed him, pulling him in for a kiss and a lengthy caress. When they parted, Henri murmured promises of returning that evening.

"Francine?"

"Never speak that name here. Here, we are Henri and Adrienne only." He sealed her protests with another kiss, and departed, smiling back at her from the door.

23

Clothed in a blue day dress, covered in a smattering of tiny, yellow flowers, Adrienne sat beneath her tree, Remi leaning into her side as she read from a primer. Taking control of the boy's educational upbringing had been met with some resistance on the part of her stubborn nephew, but he came around quickly under her firm and loving hand. She also assured him it would bring him great fortune, like his papa. This brightened the youngster's outlook considerably.

His small brow furrowed at the rows of letters and numbers. "Aunt, must I? There are so many! Perhaps we could take away a few?"

Adrienne laughed softly at his determination to end the lesson sooner. She ruffled his already mussed hair. "My sweet boy, you must learn all of them, else your conversations will be missing in meaning."

His attention was captivated by a butterfly passing by. "Oh, never. I know what I mean all the time." He lifted a hand to try and catch the flying creature, but it swerved out of his reach. "Aunt, I like it here at Beaumont. Mother never has time for me. She always has her headaches. Do you think she loves me?"

Closing the primer, Adrienne ran her hand over the embossed cover. "I am quite sure your mother loves you dearly, Remi."

Remi peered up with inquisitive eyes. "She yells so much. I had to hide. Here, I don't haf ta."

"Have to," she corrected instinctively. "Remi, you must know that I will always love you, and protect you." She embraced him, pulling the thin body easily into her arms. He squirmed, much as young boys do when held for too long. Adrienne released him, tucking away the book into her basket. "Let's forgo the lesson, shall we?" She rose, holding out her hand. "It's too hot, and I think we deserve a wade in the stream, don't you?"

Remi readily agreed, clutching her hand, all thoughts of his neglectful mother forgotten for the moment. Together, they ran to the small creek, removing their shoes. Adrienne tucked her skirts up, having allowed herself to go without proper hoops for the day. The cool water was refreshing, and Remi took many opportunities to splash her. The jubilant pair was unaware of Henri approaching on horseback.

"Papa!" Remi shrieked, stumbling up the bank to greet his parent. Henri, unable to resist the outstretched arms, swung the boy up in a circle.

Adrienne straightened her skirts, walking up the bank. "I did not think to see you back here today."

Settling the boy on his hip, Henri smiled. "I had some unfinished documents to go over." He turned his head to Remi. "Why don't you gather up your shoes and Aunt Adrienne's? I believe it's near lunchtime, yes?"

Remi wiggled down, and raced off as Adrienne lifted her chin. "You treat him with such kindness."

"He is not at fault for his mother's actions, Adrienne. Why should he suffer two loveless parents?" Henri arrogantly stole a kiss from her open mouth, stepping back as Remi returned. She blushed furiously, taking her slippers from the boy.

As they returned to the plantation house, the trio were unaware of a stealthy person lurking behind a tree. To any onlooker, they appeared a happy family. He ground his teeth in jealousy, resolving to make someone pay. As soon as it was safe, the man departed, his mousy brown hair smashed under a straw hat.

Francine's arms were akimbo as she paced the small parlor at St. Esprit. Sabine crouched in a corner, forbidden to depart unless instructed. Fleming burst through the door, ignoring the protests of house slaves trying to stop the intruding overseer. Francine glared at them and they departed, unwilling to risk possible punishment at her hands.

Fleming crossed to Francine, grasping her violently by the shoulders. "You bitch! You vile bitch!"

"Let go of me, you...cretin!" She slapped his face with such force, Fleming stepped back. "What sort of way is that to treat your mistress? I could have you driven from this house!"

"Oh, could you, *mistress*? And what would your husband think if I told him I was fucking you behind the barn, as you moaned like a whore?"

"The moaning was only for your benefit. I barely felt a thing! As for telling my husband, ha. I am sure he already suspects. Now, calm yourself." She waved her hand flippantly, and Fleming clenched his hands into fists. He had never hit a woman in his life, but the temptation was strong at that moment.

"That is my son. I could claim him."

"And reduce him to a life of abject poverty? I hardly think that would be wise. Besides, he is not my concern any longer. Adrienne has the brat now. Let her deal with his upbringing."

Fleming sneered, finally able to twist the proverbial knife. "And your husband? Is she responsible for his upbringing as well?"

Francine spun, her eyes narrowing. "Henri? His morals are too staunch to allow himself to sully his good name." She hardly believed the words, as they came from her lips. She was all too aware of the budding and growing attraction her husband had for her younger sister. Had all those years of yearning finally come to something?

"They certainly kissed as lovers do," Fleming crossed his arms, glaring at the paling woman before him.

"No!" Francine picked up a figurine, hurling it in the direction of Sabine, who yelped and dove for cover. "Never. She cannot win. She cannot have it all; Henri, Beaumont..."

"Remi?" Fleming flicked his eyes over the cowering girl. "Well, she has."

Spinning to face Sabine, Francine advanced on her, hauling the girl up by her hair. "Get me your mother, the voodoo witch. I want to curse her. I want her blood to boil out her eyes." She thrust the slave away, and Sabine ran crying from the room. Fleming turned his back to watch her go, and Francine's mind twisted. She walked to the desk, taking a letter opener in her hand.

"Dear, Isaac. You must forgive me." She crossed the room, pressing her full breasts to his back. "I spoke out of anger. I need you so very much..."

His hands fumbled back, trying to grab her body.

"I need you so very much to die," she hissed into his ear, plunging the opener into his neck with all the force she could muster.

Fleming sputtered, falling forward, grabbing at the metal implement in his neck. Francine screamed, drawing all the house slaves to her parlor. "Help! He's gone mad!"

Blood bubbled out of the overseer's neck. He gasped, trying to form some sentence as his life drained away. He pointed at her desperately, his eyes rolling back as he died on the floor.

"Miss, we should fetch Master Henri," Benji urged.

Francine played the convincing role, clasping her hand to her breast. "Yes, please! I need my husband!" The room was vacated rapidly, and she continued to sniffle until she could no longer hear voices. With a red, slippered toe, she kicked at Fleming's body, a satisfied smile crossing her beautifully cruel features.

Amidst the chaos, Clotilde entered the room, Sabine close behind. She elegantly sidestepped Fleming's body, and stood in front of Francine. "Yes, Mistress Francine?"

Lips curving upward, she met the eyes of the collected cook. "I want to put a curse on someone."

Clotilde laughed. "Curse? Mistress, I do not think you understand what you ask." Her voice was throaty, and the humor in her tone enraged Francine further.

"You will do what you say, or I will have your daughter whipped in the yard. Is that clear?" She reached for Sabine, snatching her to her side. Sabine yelped, and stumbled over Fleming's prone body.

Folding her hands at her aproned waist, Clotilde's expression sobered. "Despite your threats, you still ask..."

"Dead! I want them all dead! Henri, Adrienne...Remi...dead!" Francine screeched, her fingernails digging brutally into Sabine's arm.

"Wishing for death is a dangerous thing, mistress." Her voice was even, as she glanced at her struggling daughter. "Are you prepared to accept the conditions of such a demand?"

Francine thrust Sabine forward into the arms of her mother. "Yes. Do as I ask!"

Clotilde dipped her head into a deep curtsey, almost mocking the red-faced woman in front of her. "Yes, mistress. I will speak to you when I have fulfilled your fate." As she moved to leave, Henri burst into the room. She lowered her eyes respectfully, dragging Sabine behind her, and shutting the door.

Raising her chin to meet the burning eyes of her husband, Francine pouted. "He killed himself, Henri! It was horrible!" She flung herself at him, anger escalating as he barely touched her.

"I know what he was to you..." He pushed her upright, kneeling next to Fleming. "I feel sorrow for this man. No doubt he fell for some false charms." The storm in his eyes intensified, and Francine took a step back.

"You..."

Henri stood and advanced on her. "You think I am some foolish rube, madame? I can assure you, I am far from that! I know Remi did not spring from my loins!" He gestured with his hand to the body. "This man bears more resemblance to my son, than you or I!"

Knowing she might find herself at the end of a divorce before her vengeance could be completed, Francine decided to play at appeasing the beast before her. "He forced me, you must believe that. I could never...let a man like that in my bed."

"No, mayhap behind the barn," Henri muttered low, but loud enough for her to hear.

She let out an outraged gasp. "You dare?"

Clenching his hands into fists, he refrained from touching her. "Yes, I dare. I will overlook this. Once. Never again. I will summon the sheriff and stay to your story, but do not think I believe it for one moment." He spun on a heel and left her standing there.

Francine swallowed, pressing a hand to her abdomen, as if to flatten the already forming bump. She had thickened her skirts, wearing them higher, in a French fashion she insisted. Plans would need to be put in place to remove the baby from the home once it was born. She stared down at Fleming's body again, nudging it. She was safe, for the moment. Assured in her threats to Clotilde, she vacated the room with a satisfied smile.

24

Clotilde tugged Sabine's hand, as she walked purposefully towards the barn. The moon shone high, slightly obscured by wispy, black clouds. It looked like they were trying to snatch the orb from the night sky. The girl's legs tangled in her skirts and her body pitched forward, but she caught herself. Her muscles burned at the unusually fast pace of her mother's stride.

"Ma...Mama! Please!" she cried out, the emotional exertion of the day finally taking its toll on the otherwise composed girl.

Catching her daughter up in her arms, Clotilde stopped, gathering Sabine's trembling form into her arms. "Hush, child." They swayed under the moon. "Hush."

"Mother..."

"I know what I must do. I will make a blood

sacrifice. For your safety, and that of those under our protection." She held Sabine's head to her breast, vowing to the watching moon.

Sabine opened her mouth to speak, but found herself dragged along again, stumbling as her mother came to a halt outside the structure. She pulled the door open, ushering her daughter inside. "Light the lanterns, Sabine."

A small boy emerged from one of the stalls, rubbing his eyes. "Miz Clotilde? It be time?"

"Yes, Sam, it is."

Sabine finished her task, and stepped back as the boy retrieved a canvas sack from his sleeping palate. He held it out to her mother. "Mama say you best be sure you know what youse doin', Miz Clotilde."

"Go to her hut, Sam. Give her my thanks."

Sam's narrow shoulders rose and fell. "Yes'm." His bare feet made small indents in the light sawdust over the barn floor as he left the women. He yawned again, closing the barn door as he went.

Sabine stepped closer to her mother, watching her remove a doll from the sack. She gasped and fidgeted. "Mama..."

"Hush! You either stay and help, or go. What do you choose?" Clotilde's eyes flashed, as lantern light flickered in them. Fire danced, like they did on the ritual nights.

She knelt, giving her answer in silence. Clotilde nodded her head, removing a wrapped knife from her apron pocket. She must have taken it at great risk. A slave found with a weapon was instant death by hanging. She worried the hem of her apron, glancing at the closed door every so often.

"No one will disturb us, child. Even if they were

to try, we have precautions in place."

Sabine took comfort in her mother's smooth tone and nodded, releasing her apron and smoothing it over her legs. "What do I need to do?"

Clotilde handed her the doll and the knife. "Slice into its belly."

Taking the implements, she followed the instructions, straw emerging from the threadbare material. Clotilde threaded a needle, setting it on the ground. She removed a dirty handkerchief from her pocket. Inside its folds was a tangled mass of dark hair. Sabine searched her mother's face for confirmation this was not from their master. Clotilde smoothed the locks, twisting them into a knot, and a perfumed scent permeated the air.

She held out a hand for the knife, drawing the blade across her palm. "Baron, I call on you. In the name of my ancestors, of the faithful, of the depraved, of the lost. Hear me!" Shadows danced across the walls, and Sabine swore she saw the form of a man. "I give you this spirit. A soul black as night. A heartless woman. I ask you to take her. For this, I offer myself, a pure soul in sacrifice." Clotilde ran the hair through her blood, stuffing it into the doll. "Stitch it, Sabine!"

With unsure hands, Sabine grasped the shiny needle, repairing the rent in the fabric. Clotilde snatched the doll, smearing more blood on the face of the small effigy. She wrapped it in the handkerchief, holding her injured hand out to Sabine. She took it, feeling the warm liquid on her hand.

"My daughter. To her and her legacy, I ask protection. In your name, O Baron of Souls, I ask. I give myself." With a cry, Clotilde swooned, fainting on the floor. The lanterns went out.

Sitting straight up in bed, Adrienne's scream faded measure by measure. Strong arms enclosed her naked body, pulling her against hard flesh. "Adrienne?"

She turned in his arms, weeping, as his hands offered soothing strokes on her bare back. "It was black. I could not breathe. A man was laughing, a wicked sound."

Henri kissed her brow. "Shh. It was a dream, nothing more." He tilted her chin up, capturing her damp lips. "Shall we try to banish the memory?" His hands trailed along her sides, coming up to cup her breasts.

Adrienne fell easily into his embrace. She felt deliciously wanton, consumed by a desire she never knew before. It was as if someone was guiding her movements. She was not ashamed to direct Henri to the places she desired attention, succumbing to her own pleasure numerous times. Adrienne rocked her hips forward, meeting Henri's frantic, upward pace. She threw her head back, laughing ecstatically, the moonlight capturing her hair cascading down her back.

A voice surreptitiously permeated her mind. *Tonight, he will give you a child*. Before she could react, Henri surged up inside her, growling out his obvious pleasure at the possession of her body. She forgot the strange message, her nails digging into his broad shoulders, as his lips found hers again.

They soared high in their mutual passion, falling back to earth in measured increments, her body cradled gently against his chest.

"You are unlike any woman I have ever met. Completely unbridled in your love," Henri gasped beneath her, kissing her brow as he held her tightly. "I love you, more than my being could possibly express."

She idly traced her finger along his chest, enjoying the feel of him throbbing between her thighs. "I do not know what came over me. You bring it out in me." Adrienne could feel her cheeks heating as his hands roved down her back, grasping her buttocks possessively. She wriggled against him in a most tantalizing manner.

"Minx," he purred close to her ear.

Adrienne leaned up, staring down at his face. "Henri, what if I were...to become with child?" Worry creased her normally vibrant features.

Henri brushed back her hair with one hand, rubbing her cheek. "My love, I would consider that an honor."

"But..."

"No buts. We will cross that path when, and if, it comes. I love you, Adrienne, and if it means running away to protect you and our child, I would do it. I would abandon all I have here. I am yours, as long as you will have me."

"And Remi?" she questioned gently, not wanting to disregard the young boy she had come to care for so deeply.

Henri frowned, and she bent, kissing it away from his lips. "You are too kind, sweet woman. By law, Remi is my blood. I am allowed to take him as

I see fit."

Adrienne climbed off him, curling into his side, temporarily comforted in the thought Henri would not leave Remi to Francine's unpredictable wiles.

The following morning, Sabine carried the wrapped doll up the stairs to Francine's shadowy bedchamber. Her feet resembled lead, as she forced herself to take each step. After the ritual, Clotilde had been gravely weakened, taken in by one of the other slaves. All Sabine could understand was she was meant to take the doll to Francine, and explain she was to keep it safe next to her person at all times. The curse would be sealed, and Clotilde's desire for the protection of her family fulfilled.

Raising her hand to knock, Sabine hesitated. Long ago, she had been told by her grandmother cursing someone was wrong, even if deserved. The *loa* should only be called upon for good, helpful things. But was there ever a reason to use such black magic on a person? Sabine thought back to her overheard conversation, ordering Overseer Fleming to drown her unborn child. She shuddered, and rapped her knuckles on the door, knowing this was more than appropriate, in her mistress's case.

"Come in, damn it! Why must I be constantly plagued with these interruptions?" The harsh voice came from within.

Sabine turned the handle, and soundlessly crossed the floor to her mistress. "It is done, ma'am. My mother bids you keep this wrapped doll close so the *loa* will know what to do." The lies slipped from

Sabine's tongue, but she knew she would not fall prey to any misfortune.

The exultation that came from Francine was enough to make Sabine want to void the contents of her stomach in a chamber pot. "Oh, yes, this is wonderful! Remember my promise, girl. Should I find trickery at play, I will have you whipped within an inch of your life, while your mother watches. Is that clear?"

Hatred for this white woman coursed through Sabine's blood. She felt the calls of her ancestors, those who had fought for freedom in Haiti, crying out for vengeance. She pushed them back, unfamiliar with the new-found power surging within her. Maintaining a placid expression, she nodded. "Yes, mistress. Now, you must keep it close. Under your pillow, perhaps?" She held out a hand, offering to do the deed herself.

Francine flopped back on the bed, a satisfied smile on her lips. "Now, what can you do about my growing abdomen? I must have higher waisted dresses. Where is my husband?"

Sabine was well-aware of Henri's presence in Adrienne's bed. Little went unknown in the community amongst the slaves. "I believe he is in search of a new overseer, mistress, after Monsieur Fleming's untimely...passing."

"Business. How utterly boring. If only I were in a state to go into New Orleans!" She lay a hand over her brow. "Never mind. Be off with you. I will call if I require your presence." Francine waved her free hand idly.

"Yes, mistress," Sabine murmured obediently, shutting the door. She stared down at her soft palms, so unlike those of a field slave. She bemoaned her lack of callouses and blisters, so longing to escape the confines of this house. Mayhem was sure to befall St. Esprit before the season was out.

25

Henri sat at the familiar desk in the study at Beaumont. He had rarely returned to St. Esprit since beginning his intimate relationship with Adrienne. Knowing he was putting her in a precarious position, he began to continue writing in a leather journal, something he had not done for many years. He found the book was missing a few pages, but they were from earlier times. He concluded they must have been lost due to frequent travel.

He flipped back, remembering words he had written when he first met Adrienne. The page was gone. Frowning, he went back further, only finding his own scrawled handwriting chronicling his trip to England. He shrugged, unable to recall if he disposed of the declaration in a drunken state. Wherever they were, the page was lost to time, replaced by much happier memories.

"What is it, Henri? You look distressed." Adrienne appeared in the door, fresh as a spring breeze. Color bloomed in her cheeks, lighting her face in such a way that he smiled at her very presence.

Tucking the journal away in a pocket, he held out his hand, urging her to come to his side. She gladly acquiesced, perching on his lap. "No, my sweet. I was merely going over the accounts. Since coming into control of Beaumont, the plantation has prospered. I am pleased to say you will be well-off for many years, unless fortune demands change. In that case, you must sell everything, and move north."

Adrienne laughed, running her hand over his stubble-roughened cheek. "You, my love, worry too much. Move north? Away from all I know and love?"

"There is a rising concern in the markets...perhaps I am worrying too much." He embraced her, pulling her in for a lengthy kiss. "Where are you off to, dressed so beautifully?"

"Bessie has invited me for tea. I thought I would take Remi along to play with Louis. The boys are merely a few years apart. It would do him well to socialize with other children." She beamed at him, all her worries and concerns of the past gone from her heart-shaped face.

Henri laughed, threading his fingers through hers.

"What is it?" she pleaded, searching his face.

"Thinking of a time, madame, when you were not so...accommodating to me. I never dared believe you would be on my lap, discussing paying call to neighbors." He raised her hand, and kissed her fingertips.

"'Twas my own foolishness, Henri. Forgive me?"

Quelling his urges to make love to her on that very desk, Henri smiled. "Nothing to forgive. I believe I was rather brutish, no?"

Adrienne primly stood. "Oh yes, a horrible brute."

He laughed again. "Go now, madame. Lest I carry you upstairs, and lay you bare for my pleasure."

Coquettishly, she winked and blew him a kiss, leaving the study in a swirl of magnolia scent. He leaned back in the chair, linking his fingers behind his head, a satisfied smile on his lips. The romantic encounter would keep him sane when he had to return to St. Esprit, to run his own holdings, and possibly face Francine, as was his duty.

"Addy!" Bessie hurried out onto the porch, waving her hand as the open-topped carriage approached containing Adrienne and Remi. "It's so lovely to see you," she called out in greeting.

The carriage driver lifted Remi down, and held his hand for Adrienne, then returned to the seat to direct the horses to the stable. Bessie planted a kiss on Adrienne's cheek, and gave her a warm hug. "My, you are looking well! Being a plantation mistress seems to agree with you." She smiled at Remi. "Louis is in the parlor, I believe, with his mother."

Remi grinned, and scampered off. Bessie linked her arm through Adrienne's as they followed him into the house. "How is life at Beaumont? I so rarely see you since your father's passing. I do hope Monsieur Du Cormier is not too intolerable to have around. Although, I suppose Francine would be even less tolerable."

Adrienne giggled. "Hold your tongue, Bessie! You do have such a blunt way of speaking."

Squeezing her arm, Bessie shrugged. "I suppose that is why I have not found a husband. I told you I would be an old maid."

"By all accounts, I shall be the same," Adrienne murmured, her mind picturing being entwined with Henri in acts of love. The sobering thought dawned on her. She was his mistress in every way. Instead of shaming her, it titillated her. However, this was not Europe, nor were she or Henri nobility, by any stretch of the imagination. If discovered, she would be outcast. Her face dropped.

"Oh, Addy, what is it?" Bessie guided her to a corner suite in the parlor and sat, taking her dearest friend's hands in hers. "Has Francine done something horrid again?"

"No, she has done nothing of the sort. Surprising since I have care of Remi, but nevertheless, no, it may ruin my reputation." She lowered her voice, spying Remi and Louis playing with carved wooden animals in the corner.

Placing her fingers to her lips, Bessie contemplated her unnerved friend. "What is it?"

"You must promise never to breathe a word. Not to Sarah, nor George."

"I so swear." Bessie crossed her heart, much as they did as children when keeping silly secrets. Only this time, it was not so foolish a confidence.

"Henri..."

Adrienne scarcely had to breathe another word. Bessie's eyes shot open, and she clutched Adrienne's hands tightly. "You are his...?"

"Yes." She blushed, and lowered her eyes. "Do you think me wicked? Will you no longer invite me over for tea?"

Bessie dipped her head. "Addy, what you do is no more scandalous than me attending abolitionist meetings." She winked, most unladylike, and patted the back of Adrienne's hands. "No, I never believed Francine was right for him."

"George condones this?" Adrienne was glad to refocus the conversation on a less inappropriate topic.

Waving her hand in the air, Bessie shook her head. "I shall be a curmudgeonly old aunt, to whom no one pays any mind. And I will keep your secret, my dearest of friends."

Adrienne's relief was palatable, and she smiled warmly upon sweet Bess. "Thank you."

"Now, shall we have some tea and cakes?" She raised her voice ever so slightly, as to draw the attention of the two boys. Never ones to deny themselves sweets, they hurried to the tea tray, begging like two puppy dogs. Bessie inspected Remi. "He has flourished under your care, Addy."

Remi beamed. "Aunt Adrienne is the most wonderful aunt in the whole of Louisiana!"

All parties joined together in laughter, as the delicacies were served and devoured with zeal. For the time being, Adrienne was truly content in her life, love, family, and friends.

"Why do you carry on at Beaumont so much?" Francine walked into Henri's study, her complexion deathly pale compared to her usual countenance.

Setting aside his pen, Henri contemplated his wife. "You look quite ill. Have you seen a doctor?" He deftly avoided her first question, hoping to draw away from a lengthy conversation about his activities.

"No. It is merely a passing summer illness. Why are you at Beaumont? It cannot be because of Remi..." she simpered, coming closer to the desk.

Henri tucked aside a document. "Despite your transgressions, madame, I am still that boy's father. I will visit him as much as I like, which is more than I can say for you. Have you even given him a second thought since he departed?"

She scoffed. "Why should I? He was always whining and crying. At least my headaches have lessened. And my sister?" Francine probed, her eyes narrowing.

"Learning how to run her home very well. I will tell her you asked after her." He stood, closing his ledger, and gathering the other important papers to take back to Beaumont. "Is that all?"

Francine threw herself at him, clinging to his coat. "Stay here. I promise to be attentive." She rubbed a hand over his chest, and he stepped back in disgust.

"Madame, I would sooner sleep with the pigs!" Henri sidestepped her, leaving her standing in the study, screaming in outrage.

26

Summer gave way to early Fall, and the inhabitants of Beaumont Plantation began to look forward to the winter months. The harvest had been much more plentiful than it had been for years, and Beaumont had a healthy profit from the sale, as well as enough surplus grain to sustain them throughout the winter.

One morning, Adrienne descended the stairs to find Henri in the vast study. He was tallying the final numbers, carefully entering them into the book. His attention was immediately on her as she approached, eyes frantic.

"What is it, sweet?" He crossed to her, taking her up in his arms, murmuring words of comfort.

"Henri...I am..." Her words choked in her throat, as she sobbed anew.

He stepped back, lifting her chin. "I suspected. Please, do not cry. I am overjoyed!" He kissed her soundly, banishing all the tears instantly.

"I am so glad to hear that, Henri. Still, I worry..."

Henri swept her into a close embrace again. "Do not fret, my love. We will find the right thing to do, when the time is right. You are an uncommonly wealthy woman in your own right. Nothing will take that away." They parted when Remi's thumping footsteps could be heard coming closer.

"Aunt! Someone is here to see you!" Stepping into the room after the boy, Sabine lowered her head.

"Sabine? What are you doing here?" Henri watched the girl curiously, never fully sure of her intentions.

"I have come for Miss Adrienne. Mistress Francine wishes to invite her to visit."

Without giving much thought to her actions, Adrienne reached back for Henri, and he readily placed an arm around her waist, keeping a steady gaze on Sabine. The young slave did not flinch at the intimate gesture.

"Did my sister give a reason for her visit?"

Sabine exchanged a surreptitious look between Henri and Adrienne, before speaking honestly and plainly. "She did not say, miss."

Remi shifted from foot to foot, staring up at the adults. "Is Mother wanting to see me as well?"

Sabine reached a hand tentatively towards the youngster, but withdrew the offending limb and clutched it to her chest. "I am sorry, Master Remi. Your mother did not mention you...but she has been so desperately unwell."

Henri pulled Remi close to his side. The trio had created a sort of mock family unit over the months, yet he could see his son's crestfallen expression at the rejection of his mother's affections. "She should want to see her son. We will all go. Today."

Sabine's mouth slipped open, but she wisely shut it, curtseying. "As you wish, sir, but she wants to speak to Miss Adrienne alone." Before further questions could be asked, she scurried away, head lowered.

Henri aided Adrienne to a chair, lowering her down as she pressed a hand to her brow. Unable to voice her true feelings with Remi present, she tried to express to Henri her distress. He lay a hand on her shoulder, nodding in understanding. "Remi, return to your lessons. Your tutor will be wondering where you have gone."

The boy shot a concerned look to his aunt, but obeyed his father's command, leaving the room at once. Henri knelt before Adrienne, taking her hands in his. "She will not harm you. I have begun some arrangements. You see, I was distraught at the inability to annul my marriage to Francine. However, I have consulted with some lawyers. Due to Francine's proven infidelities, I have the ability to divorce her."

Adrienne fanned her face, peering at him uncertainly. "Surely that will cause a scandal, no?"

Henri shrugged, kissing the soft palms of Adrienne's hands. "I care not for scandal, or social mores. Hasn't Bessie already told you she will stand by you, no matter what?"

Nodding her head slowly, Adrienne recalled the wonderful conversation where Bessie committed her everlasting friendship to her, regardless of anything that happened. “Yes, but Francine will not like any of this. She will be enraged; worse than any flight of temper we have seen from her in the past!” Her blue eyes filled with tears, as she placed a hand to her still-flat stomach. “She would…”

“Never! I will never see harm come to you and my child, even if it means sacrificing my own life to keep you safe!”

“Henri, you mustn’t say such things. If it is possible, I would gladly become your wife!”

He smiled warmly, beaming up at her sweet face, before embracing her and kissing her soundly. “I will begin the proceedings immediately. For now, we must ready ourselves to see Francine. Mention nothing until I am certain of the outcome.”

While they fell into each other’s arms again with joy, their own, safe world closed in around them. The possibility for happiness was finally within grasp. Yet, neither could ignore the looming cloud, and though they rejoiced for the moment, Henri still felt the pressing weight of obligation and honor. He could only hope that Francine’s behavior was enough to back up his claims of infidelity and adultery.

Sending Sabine away on an errand gave Francine the opportunity she needed to explore Henri’s study. She knew he was hiding something. Her time to deliver her next illegitimate child was drawing near, and though she guessed the reason for Henri’s time at Beaumont, she was secretly pleased to not have to wear the constricting clothing in his absence. She bemoaned the changes to her body, and refused to eat anything but meager meals, scoffing at Clotilde. Truly, her fondest wish was for the baby to die.

Francine opened the door to the dimly lit study, closing and locking the door behind her. She moved to Henri's desk, staring at the lock. Without a thought, she grasped a small statue and bashed in the antique wood. It splintered, the drawer front falling in pieces onto the rug. She giggled with ghoulish glee, and brushed aside the remaining wood. Pulling out the papers, she laid them out on the desk, looking through them eagerly.

Most were business documents, outlining sales of crops from the plantation, and purchases of slaves. At the bottom, she discovered a letter, folded neatly. Opening the parchment, she scanned the first lines, realizing it was from a lawyer. As she read on, the word 'divorce' stuck out to her. Screeching in outrage, Francine read it again to be sure.

As of 1827, Louisiana law decrees it possible to divorce one's spouse for a number of reasons, including adultery and infidelity. As you have described, Monsieur Du Cormier, I would be certain this is a valid reason in your case...

Tearing the letter to shreds, Francine left the scraps in a pile on Henri's desk. She turned to go prepare herself for a confrontation. If Henri thought he was going to merely divorce her, thrust her aside like some old boot, he had another thing coming! Leaving the mess as it was, Francine spun and marched out of the room, hell bent on fulfilling the devious plot twisting inside her mind.

The curse was already done, she was certain. Clotilde would not dare betray her. Measures were already put in place, should things fail. The money she had covertly stolen from Henri would grease many eager palms. She groaned as the baby rolled in her abdomen, wrinkling her nose, and moving swiftly to her bedchamber. She would need to conceal the abomination growing inside her, before her sister arrived.

27

Francine had just made it up to her bedchamber, when she felt the warm seepage between her legs. Her belly constricted, and she gritted her teeth, letting out a low groan. Feeling her way to the bed, she climbed upon it, cursing everyone from Henri to Adrienne. She would never blame herself for her predicament. Everyone around her had forced her into desperate measures.

An intense fear crept into her chest, along with the next lingering contraction. Henri did not know of this second infidelity. She could not dare allow him to find out. Screaming out for assistance, a house boy came running. "Get Sabine!"

"Miss...she be gone. To Master Henri, miss...mistress!" He trembled, appearing reluctant to have answered the call.

"The cook, then! Get Clotilde, and be quick about

it!" she barked, clutching her abdomen again. The baby was early, by her count. Perhaps it would die in childbirth. Pain trickled into Francine's back, as the boy ran off to do her bidding.

She squirmed in the damp dress, hating every moment of this experience. Pushing out some squalling creature from her nether regions was far from pleasurable. The only thing keeping her centered, was the thought of shame Henri would experience. No, she would not let him divorce her, and leave her a social outcast. Fisting her hands in the sheets, she felt more liquid coming from her. Peering down, Francine realized blood was soaking through her skirts. Clotilde opened the door efficiently at that moment, and stared at the state of her mistress.

"Do not just stand there, fool! What is happening?" Francine demanded of the placid and composed cook.

"Mistress, you are in need of a doctor."

"No doctor! You! You will deliver this bastard child, and take it from my sight."

Clotilde shook her head, but set about removing Francine's sodden skirts. The blood was a worrying sign. Remembering her mother's teachings, Clotilde pressed on Francine's belly. It was taut, certainly not full term. "It is likely the babe will not survive."

"Do I care? Get it out of me!" Francine was left in a chemise, panting on the bed in agony. Her hair slipped from its carefully braided chignon, as she swore and pleaded in alternating breaths.

Sabine burst into the room, drawing back in shock. "Mama?" she asked in horror.

Clotilde kept her composure, having seen many

difficult births at her mother's side. "Boiling water, Sabine, and fresh linens. Scoot!" She pushed the open-mouthed girl from the room, and moved to Francine's side. "Let me see."

Francine clamped her legs together. "Let you what?!"

"See, mistress. I must see how the baby is progressing." Without waiting for an answer, Clotilde whipped away the remnants of the chemise, and peered down. "The babe is coming out head first. This is a good sign."

Francine cried out again. "When?"

"Mistress, how much pain were you in today?" Clotilde ignored the question from the suddenly vulnerable woman before her.

Francine shook her head. "Aches...how should I know? I've kept my stomach bound."

"You have caused your labor to come early, mistress." Clotilde clicked her tongue disapprovingly.

Growling like a cornered animal, Francine glared at the slave. "You have no right to judge your betters!"

A wave of pain struck her writhing mistress again, and Clotilde smiled inwardly. "Your sister and husband are here. Shall I call them up?"

The blood drained from Francine's face. "Get rid of them."

Clotilde nodded her head. "As you wish, mistress." She turned to address Sabine, who had returned with a basin and linens. "Please tell Mistress Adrienne and Master Henri that Madame is indisposed."

"He will ask questions, Mama..." Sabine

whispered, eyes shifting to Francine straining.

Cupping her daughter's chin, Clotilde gave her a knowing look. "Let him ask. You are clever." She kissed her brow, and Sabine left after handing over her burden. Returning to Francine's side, Clotilde frowned. "You must push. The baby needs to get out."

Francine began to thrash, clawing at the coverlet. "I want to die!"

Clotilde knelt, hiding her smile again. "I see the head. Push, mistress!"

Letting out another animal-like scream, Francine strained, and the baby's head came free in a gush of blood. Clotilde grabbed a cloth, packing it around the newborn. With the next contraction, the baby was free of Francine's body. It was feeble, letting out mucousy mewling cries. She whacked the baby on the back, freeing the clot from its mouth, and it let out a full wail. Wrapping it, Clotilde went to hand it to Francine.

"Get it away. Drown it for all I care."

Clotilde's eyes narrowed in hatred, but she said not a word. "As you wish, mistress." She knew a mother in the slave quarters who had lost a baby. "I will make sure she is cared for."

"A girl?" Francine curled into a ball. "Get Sabine to clean this mess up."

Clotilde summoned her daughter, who had returned from seeing to Adrienne and Henri. "I am taking the babe to Anna. Clean up the mistress."

Sabine inspected the child. "Poor babe."

"We will get our revenge, Sabine. Mark my words. This will not appease the *loa*." She walked down the hall, concealing the baby against her breast.

Adrienne sat before the fire, a book open on her lap. The peculiar invitation, then abrupt dismissal by her sister, played on her mind, and she could not concentrate on the words in front of her. She reread the same page several times, before shutting the book in disgust.

Henri raised his head from his own papers, crossing the room to her side. “What is it, my sweet?”

Adrienne took his hand in hers. “Do you not think it strange, what happened this afternoon?”

“Should I? Your sister’s whims change almost as rapidly as night into day.”

She secretly adored how he no longer referred to Francine as his wife. “Yes, but...” she sighed deeply. “I am overthinking things.”

Henri kissed her hand, sending shivers through her body. “I wish you would not worry so much. I will not make mistakes this time.” He got to his feet. “I need to return to St. Esprit, and retrieve some papers.”

Adrienne bit her lip, suddenly fearful. “I do not think it is wise to return tonight. Stay, and fetch them in the morning.”

He smiled, unable to resist her simple plea. “As you wish, my sweet.” He kissed her brow, letting his lips linger on her cool flesh. “Shall we retire? I have all manner of ways I wish to show you my love.”

Allowing him to draw her up, Adrienne wrapped her arms around his waist, peering up into his eyes.

"Oh, I do believe I can be persuaded."

Chuckling low, Henri scooped her up into his arms, eliciting a giggle from her. With careful steps, he bore her up the stairs and into her chamber, where they locked out all doubt and uncertainty with a click of the door.

28

"Mama! Please slow down!" Sabine reached out, clutching Clotilde's hand. They had left at sundown, walking for hours, deep into the night. "If we are caught…we will be whipped! I am sure of it!"

"Tsh! We will not be caught. Come along." Clotilde's feet followed a familiar path.

The ground sagged under Sabine's feet, and she felt moisture seep into her leather shoes. Mud sucked them deeper as she walked, envying her mother's choice not to wear anything on her feet. "Where are we going?"

"We are ensuring your safety, should I fail." Her grip tightened around her daughter's hand, as she urged her onward, deeper into the bayou. Sabine whimpered, close to tears. The past years had sucked the innocence from the young girl, having seen and done things she had never anticipated.

Sometimes, she longed for the days she ran barefoot outside, while her mother worked in the kitchens. Now, she feared for her life at the hands of a brutal white woman.

Brushing aside some vines, Clotilde ducked, and they broke into a small clearing. A man, darker than any other Sabine had seen in her life, stood by the bank, next to a raft, a rod in hand. She gasped, stepping back, but her mother yanked her forward. "Peter."

The man nodded in silent understanding, gesturing to the raft. The women boarded. Sabine leaned close to her mother, as crickets chirped and the water lapped against the wooden vessel. "Can he not speak, Mama?"

Peter looked down at her, his eyes reflecting the moonlight, as Clotilde answered, "He does not speak, nor will he. His master cut out his tongue."

Sabine shuddered, and buried her face in her mother's shoulder. The bayou was a scary place to her. She had heard stories of runaway slaves making their homes here. No white master dared to pursue them through the unknown waters, even though they declared vehemently that the rumors were false. Finally raising her head, she peered around, eyes adjusting to the darkness.

Concealed in the thick tree roots were small shacks, just like the ones on the plantation. As the raft slipped through the black waters, people watched from behind doors, and out papered windows. Sabine wondered how they survived, then she realized people like her mother must bring them food and supplies. The raft bumped against a wooden porch, and Peter helped them disembark.

“Thank you.” Clotilde reached into her pocket, handing him several bread rolls and some salt pork. Peter gratefully accepted, tipping his battered hat. He steered the raft away, after Clotilde asked him to return in an hour.

Sabine still clung to her mother, as she knocked on the shack door. A wizened voice came from within. “Who be there?”

“Clotilde.”

The door creaked open, and a hunched lady came into sight. Her teeth shone white against her skin, and Sabine gasped. “Grandmère? Mama said...”

“I know what your mama said, child. I told her to.” The old woman’s accent came from a faraway place, at least far away in Sabine’s mind. They were ushered into the shack, lit by soft lantern light. “You have grown, girl. Let me look at you.” She took Sabine’s hands in her gnarled ones. “Yes, like me when I was young.” She hobbled to the fire, removing a kettle.

Sabine stood in a state of shock. Her mother had told her the woman before them had died when she was a young child. She blinked, closing her eyes as small visions passed before them. She was looking up in wonder at the woman above her in a red shawl. The woman touched her face, and disappeared. “You ran away.”

“I did. I came here. I wanted you to come with me, but Clotilde said you were too young to be raised in darkness.” She let out a throaty laugh. “Now you live in darkness.”

“Maman, do not be cruel. How did I know she would descend on us, like the black death?”

Another rasping cough came from the old woman's chest, ignoring her daughter's question. "We could not know. The other one, though. Is it in place?"

"As you said."

Sabine shifted, questions threatening to bubble forth. "Mama?"

Clotilde exchanged glances with her mother, before finally motioning to an empty chair at the rough, wooden table. "You see, my girl, many years before you were born, your grandmère lived in Haiti, far from here. She was ripped from her family, sold to the mistress of St. Esprit. She carried with her the powers of her African ancestors, the powers we carry.

"We swore revenge, in the name of our ancestors, but the woman died. Now, she comes back in the form of your mistress," Clotilde explained, tapping Sabine on the chest.

"The *loa* come to me, even in this place. They see the youngest taken, buried alive." Her grandmère's eyes flashed. "To be saved by the kindness of another."

Sabine blinked. "Miss Adrienne?"

"We do not know. All we know is the *loa* are bent on driving your mistress mad. Even at this moment, she does not understand the things that have happened to her. They are faint dreams, possession. We have cast many, girl."

"Black magic! Mama, you said..."

Clotilde clamped a hand over Sabine's mouth. "Tsh! The free people here are very wary of the *loa*. We do what is necessary to put right fate."

Sabine shook free. "You play with fate, Mama! It

could take you from me." Tears sprung in the corners of her eyes. "Master Henri will divorce her, and send her out. The Devil laughs, Mama!" She pounded her chest. "I feel it. Black magic."

Her grandmère placed her hands on Sabine's face. "This is why we take the burden, Sabine. Look at your maman. She ages with each demand, as do I."

Sabine had ignored the fine lines gathering around her mother's chocolate brown eyes. The light was fading, all in the name of protecting her. She wept openly, her heart aching at the thought. "I must take some. Please, I beg of you."

"Never! You must survive, to guide the good light back on St. Esprit. The *loa* demand it. When they demand, we must obey." She released her granddaughter, the warmth withdrawing from Sabine's skin.

"Miss Adrienne carries a baby, the purest child of love. We must protect her, at all costs. She will suffer great loss, but will be strong. Sabine, you must be there to tend to her. We make this sacrifice so you may live."

The cries faded in her chest, as she realized what was being said. Soon, not this night, but soon, Sabine would lose her mother. "And you, Grandmère?"

"Tonight, I let my spirit pass to your mother, so she may have the strength to save those who must be saved." No hint of melancholy could be heard in her strong voice. "You carry my name, Sabine. You must be brave and strong. Many have died, but tonight, we shall ensure that you live."

Francine thrashed in her bed, a violent pain overtaking her body. She screamed, but no one came to heed her call. She cursed, and in the back of her mind, she heard a horrible voice, telling her to end her life. She was not loved, not wanted, and at that moment, her husband lay entangled in the arms of her sister.

The voice continued, pressuring her, demanding, threatening. Francine leapt from her bed, staring into the mirror of her vanity table. A strange bolt of lightning struck the sky, and a man's face appeared over her reflection. He pointed a finger, beckoning. He smiled, his teeth stark ivory against his black skin. She spun around, but there was no one in the room. Turning back, the only thing she saw was her own disheveled façade.

The pain began anew, ripping her body nearly in half. The disembodied voice returned. *You will never live to see your children grown.*

"I do not care! They are...I do not...I hate them!"

You will die. She will see to it.

Francine grabbed handfuls of her hair, pulling. "Shut up!" she cried, turning to run from the room. Tripping over a chair, she fell, curling into a ball, and trying to shut out the damning voices.

Dead...dead...dead...

29

"She is very unwell, Master Henri! Please!" Sabine's voice permeated his thoughts, as he stormed through the empty plantation house at St. Esprit.

He had found the destruction in his study, and was unwilling to let it pass as another flight of temper from his wayward wife. His letters to the parish court were drafted, outlining offenses committed by Francine, along with his wishes to divorce her on those grounds. He stated she would have a small cottage at her disposal, and Remi would continue to be under his care, only to have limited contact with his mother. He cited many religious reasons, even daring to say it would damage their son's religious health to be in contact with an adulterous woman. He was taking no prisoners this time, and his money would finally be of some use in obtaining his goals.

"Sabine, I understand your worry, and I know it is not for the woman who has so brutally abused you. You would have to come to Beaumont to care for Remi, as soon as I have settled my affairs here."

Sabine's eyes widened, and she ran away, leaving him to his search. "Francine!" He opened the door to her bedchamber, finding her curled in the bed, rocking subtly and muttering names. "If you seek to gain my affection, you will not. As you know, I have filed the necessary papers to seek a divorce."

"Divorce?" Her voice came muffled from under the sheets. She rolled over to face him, and he took a step back at her deathly pallor. Dark lines ringed her green eyes, as they stared vacantly at him.

"Have you truly gone mad, woman?" Henri thought she resembled a ghost, possessed by some unknown power. "No, I will not be swayed by childish games. You may stay at St. Esprit for the duration, but I will have no more mischief."

Francine rose from the bed, her white nightgown billowing. She flew at him, clawing at his face. He easily restrained her, calling for assistance. Two maids entered the room, and tucked their mistress back into the bed. Henri departed, tenderly feeling his cheek, and coming away with blood on the tips of his fingers.

Sabine cowered in the hallway, arms wrapped around her slim form. Henri addressed her. "What has happened? She was certainly not in this state when I last spoke to her."

"Madness, Master Henri. She was..." Sabine bit her tongue.

Henri frowned deeply. "Sabine, if you hide

something from me..."

"I...I..." She struggled for words. The years had broken down the mischievous slave girl into a trembling mess at the hands of Francine. She fainted.

Cursing under his breath, Henri scooped her up, and carried her down to the kitchens. Clotilde dropped her spoon and raced over, aiding Henri in placing her daughter in a chair. She pressed a cool cloth to the girl's face, and stared curiously at her master.

"Clotilde, you must tell me what is happening in my household. I believe in no god, but I fear something has struck down Francine with madness. I know of your rituals. Are you behind these forces?" His firm tone allowed for no disagreement from the cook as she sighed, cradling her daughter to her breast.

"You must know, Master Henri, that our people have had family brutally torn away. Babies still at the breast taken, and sold to the highest bidder. My family has been lucky, kept at St. Esprit since the time of my mother."

"I may be a white man, Clotilde, but I am not without heart. I must maintain my assets, though. What has happened in my house?" He placed a hand on the wooden table, and leaned forward.

Clotilde breathed low, murmuring to her unconscious daughter. "Mistress Francine had a baby, sir."

Henri's eyes shot wide. "A baby? What...where is this child? Was it born alive?" His heart thumped. He had not touched Francine in many months, even years. There was no way this child could have been his, but he was not about to see it suffer for Francine's crimes.

"Sir, you must understand. The baby's father was a slave. Long gone from St. Esprit now, recently sold in New Orleans."

Rubbing his brow, Henri shook his head. "Impossible. Francine showed nothing but disdain and hatred towards slaves. To let one touch her so intimately would be unspeakable. Do you think she was...taken advantage of?" A voice within his deepest soul told Henri it was silly to think Francine would allow herself in a vulnerable situation like that.

"The man said he was invited into her room. He feared no one would believe him, so he ran away from the plantation, in order to be sold."

Henri recalled such an event, eight months prior. He thought nothing of it, putting it in with the lot of owning a plantation. "And the baby?"

"Safe, sir, with her own kind. I thought it best."

Despite the gross disobedience on Clotilde's part, Henri decided she was correct. "Tend to your mistress, and say nothing of this conversation. Keep her under lock and key, do you understand?" He departed through the back kitchen door, returning to Beaumont the only thought in his mind.

When he arrived back to the plantation, Henri went to the library, knowing Adrienne would be supervising young Remi's lessons. He concentrated more when she was present, even if it was just by reading a book on the opposite side of the room. He silently entered the room, drawing only brief stares from Remi's tutor, and a toothy grin from his son. Henri moved to Adrienne's side, holding out a hand.

She gratefully took it, only giving Remi a warning stare to behave.

Adrienne followed Henri outside, and he pulled her arm through his, walking in silence. He could feel her troubled gaze on his face. The afternoon was unnaturally warm for autumn, but her blonde curls ruffled in the intermittent breeze. After walking close to the winding brook, she broke the silence. "Henri, please. Tell me what troubles you."

They stopped underneath the familiar tree, the one where the pair had shared so many chance encounters. Henri ran a hand over her face, trailing it down her arm to her abdomen, ever so slightly rounded. "I know I sound foolish, but please tell me you are true to me." His voice nearly broke, displaying an unusual amount of emotion.

Adrienne placed a hand over his. "I am true. You know this. What has caused such fleeting doubt?"

Henri leaned against the tree trunk, guiding her into his arms. "I am unworthy of such love and devotion."

"Please, I know this is unlike you. Tell me what troubles you," she pleaded again, pressing her cheek to his chest.

"You will think..."

Adrienne raised a finger to his lips, silencing protests. "I know you fear for your honor, but trust me. I only care for you, and you alone."

Faith restored, Henri told her the story of Francine and the slave, as well as the baby. He hung his head, ashamed at the conclusion of the tale. Adrienne remained silent, shocked by the brash actions of her elder sister. They sat under the tree, staring out at the water, listening to the dull buzz of insects, and the faint singing of slave workers in the distance.

When several tense minutes had passed, Henri felt Adrienne take his hand in hers. “I vow, from here on, we shall make a new beginning for ourselves. Leave Francine to St. Esprit. Let her haunt the halls. Stay here, with me and Remi. Bring the slaves over, if you must. Your plantation is cursed, my love.”

Henri acquiesced. “You are right, and wise as always. I will leave a sparse staff, but the fields will be left to overgrow, untended. I will make the arrangements.” He took in his lover’s face, noting a subtle glow in her cheeks. “You are beautiful, even more so than when I first saw you.”

“Happiness suits us both, Henri.” She lifted her chin invitingly, and he conceded, kissing her until she could no longer catch breath. Rising, he gallantly offered his hand with a mock bow, and she giggled musically. They strolled back to Beaumont, an aura of joy encircling the couple.

Francine struggled to sit up, her body throbbing, along with a dull ache at the base of her skull. She squinted around the room, and strained to hear the sounds of house slaves treading guardedly around her door. Nothing. The house was silent as the grave. She stumbled from the sweat soaked sheets on her bed. No one had tended to her. How long had she lain there?

Opening her bedroom door, she glanced into the faintly lit hall. “Sabine?” she called in the voice of a fearful child. "Sabine!" Her voice echoed off the bare walls. *Bare walls?* Francine stepped out. Many of the lavish paintings were gone from the hallway.

"Sabine!" she cried again, lifting the hem of her nightgown, and running down the stairs. She fumbled, grabbing the bannister in haste. *Where was everyone?* "Clotilde!"

The cook appeared at the bottom of the stairs. Francine stopped cold. There was something strange about the woman, stranger than she recalled. "Where is everyone?"

"Master Henri ordered us to clear the home and move, miss." Her eyes never wavered, and held a hypnotic glare. "He said you were no longer mistress of St. Esprit. You may reside here at his leisure."

Francine shrieked in outrage. "I want to see him now!" Her ebony hair hung lank around her cheeks. "And I want a bath!"

Clotilde bowed her head indifferently. "You may have those things, miss. I shall convey the message." She turned to leave, without being dismissed.

Pulling at her hair, Francine let out inhumane cries of anguish and rage. "You promised, witch! You promised they would suffer!"

Pointing a finger at the despondent woman, Clotilde laughed, a sound that made Francine take pause in her fit. "I promised there would be suffering, yes, but not theirs. There is a great plague upon this house, Francine. It lives on in you. I will not see my daughter fall prey to your whims."

"Witch! You dare speak to me in such a way?" Francine reached out a hand, and found it brutally slapped away. She held the smarting limb with genuine shock on her beautiful features.

"Death will befall you shortly." Clotilde left her simpering on the cold floor.

Francine crawled back up the stairs, feeling the energy leave her malnourished body. She managed to get back up to her bed, falling into the stale sheets. For the first time in her life, she wept with authentic sadness, regretting her choices. The voice slipped into her mind without warning. *You pathetic white girl. You had it all. Get the young one. Get her, and you will get Adrienne.*

"Yes, Adrienne. She caused all this. Too beautiful, too perfect. She is the reason for all my misfortune," Francine murmured back through sniffles.

Weak, that's what you are. You lost control.

The tears dried up, and a deep, blackened purpose took hold of Francine. She would wait. Soon, Adrienne's guilt would overwhelm her, and she would visit. The girl was too sympathetic for her own good. Francine began to laugh, and the voice chimed in, joining her in gleeful exultation.

30

With Henri and Remi at Beaumont, Adrienne began to feel as if she had her own little family back. Sabine happily assisted in the house, and the melancholy surrounding her faded almost instantly. With her help, Adrienne opened up one of the spare rooms, and began converting it into a nursery for both Remi, and the new baby. Henri surprised her with an elaborately carved rocking chair, and she was overjoyed.

The small family celebrated the Christmas holiday quietly, and they joined the slaves in a small service, avoiding the larger church. Bessie, George, Sarah, and little Louis joined the family for Christmas dinner. After, while the men shared a good brandy, the women sat in Adrienne's small parlor, conversing softly.

"Is it true he is living here? Even *I* think that is a

bit outrageous!” Sarah meant no immediate harm by her frank opinion, but Bessie swatted her on the arm nonetheless. “Ouch!”

“Oh, shush you! I know you and George were...cavorting long before the wedding day.” Bessie divulged with a flourish, causing Sarah to go bright red.

“We were honestly betrothed. Monsieur Du Cormier still has yet to get approval from the parish court.” Sarah brushed her hands over her skirt, scowling fiercely at Bessie for revealing an intimate secret.

Adrienne placed a hand over her abdomen, absently wondering what would happen if Henri did not manage to obtain a divorce from her sister. “Does the Parish speak of...?” she trailed off, knowing the two women would understand completely her probe for information.

Bessie shrugged. “Have I ever paid attention to nattering old crones? I am sure your name has been mentioned at church on occasion, but everyone in the Parish is aware of Francine’s antics. They had to be formally published along with Henri’s petition...” she trailed off, seeing Adrienne’s face drain of color. “Did you not know? Oh sweet Addy!” She hurried to her side, clasping her hand.

Sarah frowned sympathetically. “It was a shock, to know the daughter of Lord Beaumont had committed so many acts of adultery—even though some put little stock in the testimony of a slave girl.”

“Slave girl?” Adrienne quizzed, thinking there could be only one brave enough to step forward.

“Sabine, yes. Her name was in print. Henri has forever scandalized Francine’s name.” Bessie had a satisfied smile on her face.

A clearing throat drew the women's attention, as Henri and George entered the room. Bessie jumped up, hand to her throat. "Never leave women alone, George. They gossip to no end." Henri moved to Adrienne's side, deftly taking the seat vacated by Bessie.

"You must admit it is a delicious scandal. None like it that I can recall." Regaining her composure, Bessie primly perched next to Sarah, raising an eyebrow.

"It is wonderful to have progressive friends." Henri leaned back, draping an arm around the fretting Adrienne's shoulders. "There now, my dear. I only wished to spare you some of the more–delicate details of your sister's indiscretions."

George circled round, and placed a hand on Sarah's shoulder. "We presented them before the court. She has time to deny them, and provide witnesses on her behalf, but that time has come to an end. After Christmas, the parish court will rule."

Stretching out his long legs, Henri crossed them at the ankles. "Leave it to you, George, to spoil my surprise."

Adrienne perked up, a smile creeping onto her face. "Is it true?"

Turning to her, Henri clasped her hand in his, bringing it to his lips. "A rare occurrence, my dear, but true. If I have my way, we will be married in early spring."

Her mouth forming a little 'o,' Adrienne blushed furiously in front of her dearest friends. "Perhaps...sooner?"

"Sooner? Addy, darling, there is no reason to

rush, unless…" Bessie gasped, as she realized the full extent of the situation. "Oh my!"

George was grinning, glad to see his friend so happy. "You should not let this news beyond this room, despite its joyous nature. For the moment, the Parish is content in the exposure of Francine's non-virtuous actions. No reason to taint your name further. Although no one speaks of it, of course." Congratulations were given all around, and the five celebrated the holiday long into the night.

Later, when Adrienne was finally abed with Henri, he lay on her bare breast, tracing his fingers along her rounded stomach. Both were sated from frantic lovemaking, basking in the afterglow.

"Do you think the baby is a boy or a girl?"

Adrienne looked down on him with adoration, watching his child-like expression. "I should like a girl, although I know most men wish for a boy."

"No, we have Remi. I should like a girl. There will be plenty of time for another, and another." He kissed her stomach possessively, drifting lower, and placing feathery kisses along her bare thighs.

Adrienne moaned softly, running her fingers through his tangled hair. "Ohhh, I do not know if I can take more adoration at your…"

His deft fingers parted her damp folds, and her hips arched up as his tongue found its mark. She let out a breathy sigh, ending with his name. He strummed all the nerves of her sensitive body until she could no longer bear it, and when he entered her, they cried out in mutual pleasure. Henri brushed away her curls, beholding her beautiful face as he loved her, possessed her, and drowned in her sweet kisses.

"I will always love you, Adrienne. My promise to you." He pushed into her body a final time, allowing himself to be completely consumed with her undying passion.

Sabine crept past her master and mistress's bed chamber, swallowing hard in embarrassment at the last sounds of their lovemaking. She rubbed her burning cheeks as she passed, ashamed to be disobeying their direct orders, but she had to see her mother. It was the first time, in all Sabine's life, that she had not been with her on Christmas. They would perform a ritual for luck in the coming year, and give small tokens, despite poverty.

She held the handkerchief close to her breast. Mistress Adrienne had taught her to embroider, and she had carefully stitched the magnolia flower and her mother's name under the instruction of the kind lady. She was bound and determined to give it to her mother this night. Retrieving her new woolen shawl, and wiggling her toes into her new boots, Sabine cozied herself against the bitter cold evening and threatening snow. She left through the kitchen, sneaking around a sleeping Helene. The woman was kind, but she made no replacement to Sabine's own mother.

The night air was crisp, and her breath made puffs of white, as she walked the familiar path to St. Esprit. Her life at Beaumont was exponentially better. No more beatings, happy sounds of Remi playing, and the kind, but firm guiding words of Mistress Adrienne. Master Henri forbade the slaves from St. Esprit to return to their former homes, and none were reluctant in obeying. Life at Beaumont was good, unlike many plantations nearby.

Her boots crunched on frozen leaves, as she rounded the drive to the dark plantation house. It was nearly abandoned. Sabine did not understand why her mother decided to stay, but she reckoned it had something to do with protecting her. She rounded the house to the kitchens, opening the creaking back door.

The coals in the stove burned low, a flickering orange, then red. It should have been a warning sign to Sabine. She called out low. "Mama?"

There was no answer, then, darkness.

31

Henri descended the stairs to the dining room shortly after ten, invigorated by his night with Adrienne. He found Remi sitting, fiddling with his bowl of porridge, still dressed in his nightshirt.

"Son, where are your clothes?"

The small boy raised and lowered his narrow shoulders. "Sabine wasn't there to wake me, Papa. I came down 'cause I was hungry. Not so much now." He raised his spoon, wrinkling his small nose as the glop dripped down.

Sitting next to him, Henri tried to ignore the uneasy feeling drifting into his chest. "Did you ask Helene?"

"Mmhmm. She said Sabine ain't here." Remi took a tentative bite. "Can I have some sugar?"

Henri mindlessly pushed the bowl over. "Not too much." He returned the boy's toothy grin, ruffling his hair.

Scooting back the chair, he headed back up the stairs to Adrienne. She was curled in the sheets, hair delicately draped over one bare shoulder. It was tempting to forgo his questions and take her again, but he refrained. "Adrienne?" He touched her brow, and her blue eyes flickered open. "Did Sabine say she was going anywhere?"

"Hmm? No, I do not think so."

"Would she go back to St. Esprit? To see Clotilde, maybe?" Henri urged.

Adrienne blinked, comprehending what he was implying. She sat up, modestly clutching the sheet to her body. "I did tell her not to go alone. You do not think—"

He grimly nodded. "Stubborn girl!"

Moving close, Adrienne placed a hand on his face, turning to toward her. "We should search for her first, before drawing conclusions."

He kissed her brow. "Sensible to a fault, my love. I will call Benji, and have him make a search of the slave quarters, as well as the rest of the house. Please come join us for breakfast, lest I am tempted again to take you to bed." He tugged at the flimsy sheet, revealing a crested nipple to his gaze.

Adrienne swatted his hand, but he could not deny the worried expression in her eyes. "Shoo, and I shall! I do hope Sabine has simply overslept somewhere."

"As do I, love."

Sabine raised her head groggily, realizing she was

bound to an elegant, curved arm chair in Francine's bedchamber. Her body hurt all over, and it dawned on her that she had been dragged up the stairs. The room was dusty and dark, and had a musty smell. She wrinkled her nose, trying to make sense of the shadows around her.

"She awakes! Like from some fairy tale. You always had such a high opinion of yourself, for a slave!" Francine appeared in her line of vision, and Sabine gasped. The creature before her surely could not be the Southern mistress she had left not two months past. Her hair hung loose, unwashed, and she wore a white, stained nightgown. She circled in front of Sabine, holding a lantern high. She had aged considerably, wrinkles crisscrossing her once smooth skin.

"Mistress Francine, what happened?"

The slap came with brutal strength, snapping Sabine's head back. "Shut up! I am stunning. He said I would have my beauty back."

Tasting coppery blood on the inside of her mouth, Sabine toughened her resolve. "My mother?"

She danced wildly in front of Sabine, like some sort of banshee. "She stayed...thought she would be powerful, but she was wrong. So very wrong. I locked her in the cellar days ago." Sabine caught sight of the basement key, dangling on a thin chain around Francine's neck.

More gleeful dancing followed, while Sabine stared in abject horror. Her mind raced, trying to sense her mother in some way. She must be still alive. Sabine would know if she passed. When her grandmère had taken her life in the swamp with her mother's knife, she had felt the stabbing pain. She felt no such pain coming from her mother's soul, but she remained silent.

"You will bring Adrienne to me, or I will make sure your mother dies." Francine pulled out an object that glinted in her lantern light. A knife. "I will cut out Adrienne's heart, and feed it to Henri!"

This was madness, the kind Sabine had feared when her mother had given in to the dark arts. She pleaded not to offer souls to the *loa*, but her mother was determined to protect her family from this. Now, the creature stood before her, unhinged from her very senses. Sabine nodded her head, hoping agreeing would buy her some time to formulate a plan to save her mother.

"Good. You will make a blood vow."

What did this white woman know about blood vows? "Mistress, I..."

Before Sabine could react, Francine swiped the knife over her arm, and the thin line reddened, smarting fiercely. She wiped her hand through the blood, and rubbed it on her face. "You swear!"

Mentally begging and pleading to all the spirits of her ancestors, and all the gods, Sabine prayed they would understand, and not hold her to her vow. "I so swear."

Francine raised the knife again, and Sabine cried out, sure she was going to die. Instead, her bonds were cut. "Tonight...bring her tonight, or your mother dies."

Sabine stumbled, wanting to get out of the cursed place as quickly as possible. Her departure was punctuated by manic laughter, and when she dared to glance back, Francine was at the top of the stairs, waving the lantern wildly.

"Sabine! Where on earth have you been? We have been worried sick." Adrienne set her needlework aside, as the breathless girl burst into the library. Remi peered up inquisitively at her arrival, a wooden animal in his fist.

Sabine curtseyed. "Apologies, mistress. I lost track of time, you see."

"Did you not hear the men calling? Henri went out hours ago with a search party. You must realize how dangerous it could have been, had you come across anyone." Adrienne folded her hands in her lap.

"Yes. I am sorry. I...I had a note from my mother. Your sister is very ill, and has asked for you." Sabine bit her lip, and twisted her apron in her hands, disgusted by the lie. Mistress Adrienne was a good lady, protected and loved. "She said it is a desperate time."

Adrienne stood. "I should speak to Henri first."

"No! I mean, no, mistress. There is little time." Sabine thought only of her mother, possibly hurt, lying on a cold basement floor. She ignored the voice telling her that Clotilde would have made the sacrifice to see her pact fulfilled. "I shall stay with Remi."

Hesitating, her mistress's kind heart compelled her to see Francine, and seek forgiveness. "Very well. Please inform Henri, and tell him to join me as soon as possible." She summoned her maid, who brought her a cloak, staring at Sabine suspiciously.

Hetty ushered her mistress to the carriage. "Should I find Master Henri, mistress?"

"No, I am sure it will be fine. My sister is sick. I should return by the evening." Adrienne smiled, trying to reassure the maid, as she gestured to the coach driver to go.

Sabine watched nervously from the library window, touching the cold glass. *What had she done?*

Pulling off his coat, Henri groaned, rubbing the back of his neck. Riding in the cold most of the day, searching for Sabine, had taken a toll on his muscles. Thinking only of seeing Adrienne, he headed to the library. Remi was curled up on one of the chairs, thumb in his mouth, asleep. No one else was around.

Deciding his best option was to wake the boy, Henri knelt down, shaking Remi by the shoulder. "Remi? Where is Adrienne?"

Sleepily, the thumb popped out of his mouth, and he squinted up at Henri. "Went to see Mother."

"Mother? Your mother?" Henri rocked back on his feet, standing. "Remi, are you telling me the truth?"

The small head nodded. "Sabine came, and said Mother was sick. Is she sick, Papa?"

"Sabine?" Henri rubbed his brow, feeling the tension rising in his head. "She came here?"

"Yes, to tell Aunt Adrienne Mother was sick, and she had to go right now. Auntie wanted to tell you, but Sabine said it was...ungent." His lips tried to form the unfamiliar word.

"Urgent?"

"Yeah." Remi yawned. "Can I go see her?"

Henri ran to the door, throwing it open. "Benji!" he hollered out, causing the old slave to come at a jog.

"Yes, suh?"

"Get my horse. I need to go to St. Esprit right away. Did you know Adrienne had gone?" He drew him out into the hall, away from Remi's prying ears.

The man shook his head. "No, Master Henri. I've only just returned with you."

Henri nodded, retrieving his coat. "Yes, of course. How silly of me."

"Should I send men along after you?" Benji must have seen the strain in his master's eyes.

"Yes, I think it might be necessary. I fear Adrienne is in terrible danger. Make sure someone looks after Remi." Moving back into the library, Henri took his pistol from the desk drawer. The flintlock was somewhat more cumbersome than he would have liked, but it would provide distraction, if necessary. With his horse saddled, he set back off to St. Esprit, fear filling his heart.

32

The full moon lingered in the frostbitten sky, the horses' breath coming in puffs of white steam. The carriage driver asked Adrienne if she wanted him to accompany her into the house, but was visibly relieved when she declined. He was more than happy to go stable his horses. Adrienne climbed the creaking steps, St. Esprit a looming shadow against the backdrop of night.

A gust of cold air swept across the abandoned porch, swirling unswept dirt around Adrienne's ankles. She shivered, reaching out to knock on the massive door. Instead, it swung open, letting out a horrendous groan. Her heart momentarily ached to think of her sister in such squalor. She was used to the finer things in life. Adrienne wondered how Henri could leave her desolate, but she remembered how she had slighted him, unforgivably.

Vases balanced on pedestals alongside the stairs, the flowers dead, petals having drifted to the floor. Adrienne rubbed her arms against the cold. An overwhelming feeling of dread enveloped her, and she touched her distended abdomen with worry. Drawing in a breath, she called out for her sister in the dark interior.

Another gust of air rustled her skirts, and she spun, searching for the source. The door slammed shut behind her, and she let out a cry, stumbling forward to the stairs. Grasping the bannister, she looked up. A glow came from the top of the stairs, emanating from a side hallway. Adrienne clambered up the steps, ignoring the force pulling her back.

"Francine? Are you up here? Clotilde?" she tentatively spoke up. Her reply was a low laugh in the distance. "Francine? Is that you?"

The door to her bedroom was cracked open, and light trickled out into the hall. Adrienne clutched her cloak tighter, taking carefully measured steps toward the door. She pressed a hand to the wooden portal, pushing it fully open. "Francine?"

A figure lay on the curtained bed, light shining through from a candle perched on a dressing table. Adrienne moved over quickly, drawing back the covering. She gasped, eyes searching the sheets for the sign of a real person. Pillows and blankets provided the shape she had witnessed.

"Dear little sister..." Francine's eerily haunting voice had her spinning around. The woman's cold hands came around her throat with ease, and the pair fell back, tearing down the curtains on the bed.

Adrienne struggled, trying to dislodge her sister's fingers, as they choked the breath from her.

Her cloak fell away in the fray, and Francine jumped back, seeing her sister's swollen stomach.

"And he dared call me a whore? For the entire Parish to hear?" She threw her head back, grating laughter emerging from her pale lips. "You are the whore, sister. How soon did you spread your legs? No better than I!"

Gasping for air, Adrienne pushed herself to her feet, rubbing her neck. "I love him, which is more than can be said for you!" A white, burning energy filled her body, and she knew she had to fight to survive.

Francine paced the room like a caged beast, muttering to herself. She was bordering the edges of sanity, and Adrienne watched in horror. She tried to make a move to the door, but Francine flung herself across it, something sharp and glistening in her hand. "He left me here, you know. Said he cared not if I rotted!"

Adrienne shook her head, not believing Henri could be so callous and cold to her only blood left. "Francine, let me help you. We can get you a cottage, and you will have peace."

"Peace? With him screeching in my head for blood?" She gestured with the pointed object to her temple, and it was then Adrienne saw it was a sharpened letter opener.

Holding out her hands in a gesture of futility, she tried to appeal to the humanity she hoped still lurked in her sister. "Think of your son...he needs his mother..."

"Ha! Mother? Nay, you are his mother now, *dearest sister*." Francine held the makeshift weapon at arm's length. "You are a witch! You and the one I have locked in the basement. Cursed!" She advanced, waving the letter opener in the air.

Adrienne screamed as Francine leapt forward. She crouched by the bed, protecting herself from the advancing fury, and covering her ears. The fatal blow never came. Instead a shot reverberated in the small room. Adrienne let out a whimper as Francine stumbled, turned, and faced her adversary head on. She brandished the rudimentary weapon, making contact with Adrienne's savior. However, the shot was true. Francine crumbled into the arms of the man she had sworn to hate for eternity.

Henri cradled Francine in his arms for a moment, before placing her weeping form on the bed. He hurried around and lifted Adrienne into his arms, soothing the terrified woman with gentle kisses. "It's over now."

A wheezing laugh came from the woman on the bed, blood trickling out of the corner of her mouth. "Yes, he's calling me."

"Why, Francine? We were never happy together. It was better for it to be like this. And you have killed before," Henri gently scolded. "I would have provided for you, regardless of the outcome."

"She always wins, doesn't she?" Francine fixed her reddened eyes on Adrienne. "You might have lost this time, but you had help." She clasped a hand over the bloodied gown. "She betrayed me." With a final inhale of breath, Francine died with a rattle.

Sabine appeared at the doorway, hand clasped over her mouth. "Miss...I...my mother..."

Henri spied the gold chain around Francine's neck, and removed it. He handed the key to Sabine, who sprinted from the room. He turned to Adrienne again, brushing her hair back. "Sabine explained it all. She thought Francine would kill her mother, and so she tricked you into coming here. She's deeply sorry, but..."

She pressed a finger to his lips. "No more excuses. We live now for today."

Sabine returned, supporting her mother. Clotilde took in the scene with disgust. "Burn her."

"What?" Henri spun, staring in horror.

Clotilde, even in her weakened state, limped to the vanity table, picking up the candle. "I made a vow. Leave, now! Or I will take us all with her."

Henri, not knowing what madness the voodoo queen possessed, scooped Adrienne up in his arms, and hurried from the room. "Sabine, now!" He stared at the young girl frozen to the spot.

"Sabine, this is how it must be." Clotilde threw down the candle, and the bed was rapidly engulfed in flames. Sabine stepped back with a scream. "I love you, daughter. My promise is kept. A soul for a soul."

The heat of the flames intensified, catching the rug and advancing towards Sabine.

"Sabine, move!" Henri shouted from the stairs, and Sabine sobbed as she left her mother to be consumed by the inferno.

Once outside, Henri's men rode up, led by Benji, but it was too late. Flames licked the night sky, the plantation house burning, even in the cold winter air. The wood cracked, and the roof caved in. Sabine tried to run back, but Henri caught her by the waist, passing her off to Benji. St. Esprit was no more.

33

January, 1841

Henri sat at his desk, making a few final notations in his leather bound journal. As he penned the final word, Adrienne slipped in with a subtle smile. "Remi is asleep." Henri gestured for her to come closer, moving back his chair so she could sit on his lap. He held a hand possessively over her stomach, pleased to feel his child kick.

"And you? How are you, Madame Du Cormier?"

Adrienne giggled at the formal name. "Well. *We* are well." She placed a hand over his. "What are you doing?"

"Well, one day, Remi is going to ask me what happened to his mother. I found it a gentler idea to let him think his mother died due to fever."

Kissing him sweetly, Adrienne nodded, unable

to stop a small tear trickling down her cheek. “How kind to my sister, even with all her ill behavior towards you.”

“You more than make up for all the hardships I've had to endure.” He thumbed the tears away. “Now, please stop shedding tears. Things have all worked out for the best.”

The couple embraced again, the fire crackling merrily in the hearth, and the cold winds locked out for good.

Sabine left Beaumont under the cover of night, making her way to the graveyard, and Francine Du Cormier's freshly laid tomb. Henri gave her a burial fitting a mistress of a plantation, and although the Parish mourned, no one truly missed the woman's unpredictable ways, least of all the slaves.

She was met by several men, who pushed aside the stone covering the grave, to reveal a set of stairs. The trio descended into the depths of the Du Cormier crypt. In the small room beneath the crypt, Clotilde stood, smiling warmly at her daughter. Sabine rushed into her open arms.

“You will protect those who need it now, daughter. I will retreat into obscurity.”

Sabine nodded, hugging her mother again, peace flowing through her body. Even in the dark cavern, a tinkling laughter could be heard, followed by, *Bonne chance, petite.*

The End

Historical Note

Louisiana Voodoo, also known as New Orleans Voodoo, during the 1830s and 1840s on slave plantations is cloaked in mystery. It came about in the 1700s, when many slaves were transported to the colonies from West Africa. We believe it originated mainly with the Fon people, from what is now the Republic of Benin. Many voodoo rituals carried elements of Catholicism, but also focused on ritual creation of charms and amulets.

The *loa*, almost the equivalent of Catholic saints, were not only worshiped, but served. Each had distinct personalities and desires. For example, Mademoiselle Charlotte, mentioned in this novel, was based on a white mistress at a plantation. She spoke mainly French, and was hard to please, and only worked for people she fancied. She evolved from Haitian voodoo.

When the Embargo Act of 1804 ended the importation of slavery to the United States, however, there were many voodoo queens in Louisiana and New Orleans. Many earned their living dancing and selling herbs, and some experienced unprecedented freedoms in the Deep South. By 1840, even with the embargo, New

Orleans was the biggest slave trade port in the United States. Slavery in the United States would not be abolished until Abraham Lincoln's Emancipation Proclamation of 1863.

Voodoo practices still remain as a fascination even to this day. New Orleans has many museums dedicated to the practice, and the thriving tourist industry has capitalized on the trend. The New Orleans Historic Voodoo Museum houses many artifacts, and still performs rituals and blessings to this day.

Note

Thank you for reading *Bitter Bonds*. The idea for this novel stemmed from an unexplored storyline in my Rae Hatting Mysteries series book *Misfortune*. It blossomed from there, the characters evolving into a life of their own. I have done my best to remain true to the time period, twenty years before the American Civil War. If you have enjoyed the novel, please consider leaving a review.

Be sure to check out some of my other books, including *The Soldier's Secret* and *Misfortune*, Book 2 in the Rae Hatting Mysteries!

Find me on Facebook at:
https://www.facebook.com/HAOsborne

To keep up with information about upcoming releases, please subscribe to my newsletter for a free book! http://bit.ly/HeatherOsborneNews

About the Author

Heather Osborne was born and raised in California. She has a Bachelor of Science in Criminology and Victimology, as well as coursework in Early Childhood Education. In 2009, she moved to Scotland. Heather has been writing short stories for as long as she can remember. She also has written and directed several plays. In her spare time, Heather enjoys reading, writing (of course!), theatre, as well as caring for her young son.

www.ingramcontent.com/pod-product-compliance
Lightning Source LLC
LaVergne TN
LVHW040138291025
824529LV00021B/150
* 9 7 8 1 5 3 0 1 3 9 3 2 3 *